Claybore's scream ripped through Lan's flesh, made his skin crawl and gave him sensations of taste unknown to him before. But his fingers brushed the pink, soft Sphere. The Kinetic Sphere "fell" sideways, slowly at first, then it vanished through the thick walls of whiteness.

"You fool!" shrieked Claybore. "You unutterable fool! I need that!" The sorcerer turned taloned fingers toward Lan, but the brief separation from the Sphere aleady worked deadly changes. The mage's skin rippled and began to drip like water from a melting icicle. Even as Lan watched—smelled—Claybore's flesh washed away, leaving behind only a hideous skeleton.

THE SORCERER'S SKULL

ROBERT E. VARDEMAN

ACE SCIENCE FICTION BOOKS
NEW YORK

THE SORCERER'S SKULL

An Ace Science Fiction Book / published by arrangement with
the author

PRINTING HISTORY
Ace original / June 1983

ISBN: 0-441-77541-1

Ace Science Fiction Books are published by Charter Communications, Inc.
200 Madison Avenue, New York, New York 10016.
PRINTED IN THE UNITED STATES OF AMERICA

For Kerry
AND THE WORLDS
THAT MIGHT HAVE
BEEN . . .

CHAPTER ONE

Lan Martak screamed in silent agony. The world shifted and turned to soft white all around. His words rattled and fell like tiny pebbles, but he didn't hear them, he *saw* them. He reached out, cut his finger on them. The dripping blood wasn't seen as much as it was *tasted*. His senses were jumbled and confused.

Sight, taste, smell, hearing, touch, all changed in a bewildering kaleidoscope. Lan heard himself falling, tasted the impact against velvet, heard the dim outline of someone near.

"Lan!" came the cry. "I'm frozen solid. Help meeeee!"

"Inyx!" He fought to order the universe, failed. Lan worked toward where the woman had been and found himself wrapped in down-soft clouds of vapor. He sought her. He didn't find her.

For an eternity he staggered, senses altering in some unknowably random fashion. He felt his brain turn to liquid fire, *things* crawl through it, other *things* change within him. The occasional times he heard with his ears, saw with his eyes, felt with his fingers, he made slow progress. But to where?

The Kinetic Sphere had opened a gateway unlike any of the natural cenotaph roads between worlds he'd taken before. He was reminded of the maze he and his companions had followed in Waldron's dungeons, yet this limbo contained none of the obvious physical dangers. If anything, the subtle danger was greater—to spend the rest of eternity with shifting senses would drive him insane. At least, Waldron's dungeons contained dangers he could see and fight. And his friends, the dark-haired Inyx and the gigantic, towering, talking spider Krek, had been there to aid him against the would-be conqueror's minions.

Here, he fought a lonely battle, an ever-changing one. He tasted roughness. His eyes heard a familiar voice.

"You thought it so easy to use the Sphere?" Demoniacal laughter accompanied the taunt. Claybore appeared in the soft fog, miraculously whole of body but still sporting the fleshless skull. The eyeholes burned with ruby fury. The last time Lan had seen the decapitated sorcerer had been seconds before he, Inyx, and Krek had walked along the Road opened by the Kinetic Sphere, that wonderous device fashioned and lost to Waldron— or so he said—by Claybore. "That buffoon Waldron knew nothing. I used him. Now that I have regained the Sphere, nothing will prevent my conquering the entire universe, one world at a time."

"Claybore?" Lan called, uncertain. The spectral figure shimmering in the fog held a pinkly pulsating globe in one hand: the Kinetic Sphere.

"Who else? I am a sorcerer supreme! Now my plans can be put into full effect."

"You're responsible for the grey-clad soldiers?"

"I used Waldron for that purpose. Many are his men. But they obey *my* commands! They will flood all the worlds along the Cenotaph Road and conquer at my behest. I will rule!"

"Where are we? What happened?"

"We are nowhere, in a world between worlds. The instant of transport is critical. After making certain that Waldron was properly exiled back to his own bleak prison world, I altered the chant at the last possible moment to give you this little excursion, to give you a taste of what it means to cross a master sorcerer."

Lan's initial panic subsided. While he was far from accepting the cavalcade of sensory changes torturously twisting around him, it no longer frightened him. His mind calmed; he forged a plan. He acted.

Claybore's scream ripped through Lan's flesh, made his skin crawl, gave him sensations of taste unknown to him before. But his fingertips brushed the pink, soft Sphere. The globe rose up as he touched it and obeyed a gravity vastly different from anything Lan had imagined possible. The Kinetic Sphere "fell" sideways, slowly at first, then with increasing velocity. In the span of a heartbeat, it vanished through the thick walls of whiteness.

"You fool!" shrieked Claybore. "You unutterable fool! I *need* that!" The sorcerer turned taloned fingers toward Lan, but the brief separation from the Sphere already worked deadly changes. The mage's skin rippled and began to drip like water from a melting icicle. Even as Lan watched— smelled—Claybore's flesh washed away, leaving behind only a hideous skeleton.

Then the bones crumbled like chalk until only the skull floated in the billows of fog, malevolent ruby beams lancing outward to be absorbed by the cloaking white.

"Lan Martak, I shall punish you for this! I shall make you cringe, grovel, beg for death. Then, *then* the pain shall truly begin for you. I shall keep you alive for eternity, every instant one of excruciating pain. I shall . . ."

Claybore's voice faded. Thick blankets of swirling fog surrounded his skull and hid its horrible visage from sight. Lan again existed alone in the limitlessness of limbo.

"Claybore!" he called out, hands groping for the sorcerer's skull. Even the promise of eternal damnation offered by the mage seemed better than wandering alone and lonely in this infinite fog.

Fingers caressed his arm. A voice spoke. Truly spoke.

"Lan, you are with me. I never thought you'd follow. . . ."

"Zarella?" The shock of again hearing the voice of the woman he'd so foolishly loved sent his heart racing. She came to him from eons before—before he had been forced to flee his home world due to the pursuit of the grey-clad soldiers, before his half-sister had been raped and murdered, before he had walked the Cenotaph Road and found true friends in Krek and Inyx. "Where are you? How did you survive? Surepta killed you!"

"Yes, Surepta and his grey soldiers killed me," came the lament. "I wander this world now, waiting."

"For what?"

It was as if Zarella did not hear him.

"I am like the *therra*, though I can never return to my body. I meet many here, learn what happens at the Dancing Serpent. All is well there. They do not even miss me. The gambling goes on, the drinking is never-ending, even the old sheriff occasionally stops in to quiet the crowds, though there is little need of him now that the town is totally under the power of the interloper soldiers."

"Zarella, I miss you!"

"More than I'd've thought, dear Lan. To follow me as you've done shows either true love—or stupidity."

"There are others with me. Can you find them? I can't tell where I am, nor can I believe my senses."

"That is because you still possess a body. Cut

loose, a spirit or *therra*, there is no resistance to the fog. I can see . . . forever."

"Can you find a spider, a large spider? And a woman with dark hair?"

"Another woman?" came Zarella's mocking voice. "Yes, I see another still in body. And the spider." Her voice became wistful. "A huge spider, yes. In life I feared them. Now that I've lost all there is to lose, I fear nothing."

"Can you help us? Please, Zarella."

"What? No protestations of love? Can it be you've truly learned my true nature?" Her voice carried the old tinge of sarcasm, but it was now softened by . . . something. Lan Martak dared hope it was love, for him, for humanity, for the mortal life he and his friends represented.

"That you can love no one but yourself? Zarella, I suppose I always knew that, but you were so beautiful. The most gorgeous woman I've ever known."

"Including this dark-haired woman warrior?"

"Yes."

"You touch my vanity. My spirit is indistinguishable from thousands of others I've encountered in this horrid nothing place. To hear a mortal again tell me of my beauty is a gift beyond compare. Turn right. Walk."

Lan felt ghostly fingers on his shoulder. Only tendrils of fog touched him. He reached out, put his hand on top of them. The tendrils became more substantial, warmer, almost human. He heard a very human sigh.

Then, "Here is one of your friends, Lan, my darling."

"Krek!"

"I see you have found an acquaintance," said the spider petulantly. "You humans possess the most peculiar abilities. This fog completely befuddles me. I 'see' the Kinetic Sphere, but it is so distant and grows more so with every passing instant. And, of course, I see the wraiths."

"The woman. Do you see Inyx?" demanded Lan, feeling the pressure of time working against them. He felt his senses slipping, as if the longer they stayed in this dimension, the harder it would be to leave. To be trapped like Zarella, disembodied and longing a return to life, didn't appeal to him. Since her death back on their home world, he had learned much. He wanted to live, really live.

"She . . . she is so distant; she blunders away. But I 'see' the Sphere. To the left." Krek loomed half again taller than a man, eight long legs coppery and gleaming in the mist, the only substantial anchor in shifting whiteness.

"I don't see it," Lan said. He possessed a slight magic-sensing ability and some facility with minor spells, but nothing more, while Krek's "vision" spotted both the cenotaph roadways to other worlds and the Kinetic Sphere with unerring accuracy.

"I do. It . . . it's your way out of this dimension," said Zarella almost wistfully. Lan didn't have to be able to read her mind to know what the ghostly creature thought. If Lan were stranded here, she wouldn't walk the roads of forever alone.

"Zarella," he started, but she cut him off. The tendrils tightened on his shoulder, almost as if they were real, womanly, human fingers.

"You loved me and I spurned you. I can now give you a gift to repay what I could not in life." The touch vanished from his shoulder.

"What're you doing, Zarella?"

"Good-bye, Lan. Think of me."

He felt a damp breeze over his lips, then somersaulted over and over—to land hard enough on solid earth to knock the wind from his lungs. Krek loomed over him as he gasped, trying to regain his breath.

"We seem to have arrived safely, friend Lan Martak," observed the spider. "Wherever this is."

Lan struggled to sit upright. The terrain stretched out green and inviting with more than spring, but less than summer, in the air. No hint of the white fog remained. They truly found another world along the Cenotaph Road, a substantial world, not one of indeterminate dimension.

"Inyx!" he cried. "Where's Inyx?"

"Nowhere I see. You feel we should seek her out?"

"Krek, of course I do!" Lan had made many mistakes in his choice of women, unwisely loving Zarella, being ensorcelled by another, but his feelings for Inyx were true. He hadn't sorted them out to his own satisfaction. Perhaps it was love, perhaps only duty. But above all, he was responsible for their walking the Cenotaph Road using Claybore's Kinetic Sphere. And, in a lesser way, he had caused Inyx to become lost when he batted the Sphere from the sorcerer's hand within the misty limbo he and Krek had just left.

"Hmmm," said the spider, rubbing two front legs together in thought, "your choice in females is improving. I am rather taken with Inyx also." The spider turned around and around, then performed a curious hopping motion. "I 'see' only one cenotaph on this world. It must be high atop a mountain."

"But Inyx!" protested Lan.

"Since we do not know this world, where else are we most likely to find her?"

"You're right. It's the only logical place, if she's on *this* world. But what if she dropped into some other world?"

"Possible, but not likely. We went into the mist together. It is highly likely we left it together.

There are bonds between us not easily broken, even by such an interworld journey. I have the feeling Claybore is also on this world."

"Claybore," said Lan, his voice hardening. "With the Kinetic Sphere, he'll rule the entire Cenotaph Road."

"Perhaps he does not have the Sphere. Perhaps the potent cenotaph I 'see' *is* the Sphere. I cannot tell. We must get closer. At least having mountains around me will be a pleasant change. I find this flat country so tedious."

"This appears to be a kindly world for one as old and infirm as myself," said Krek.

The trilling words came with a modicum of animation now. The spider rejoiced in his own way of being free of his home world and his overamorous bride, Klawn-rik'wiktorn-kyt. Lan had helped the lovelorn spider return to his web for mating, not discovering until later that Krek's bride was obligated to devour her mate afterward. Krek had betrayed almost human traits in not liking this outcome and had rejoined Lan Martak to walk the Cenotaph Road. But genetic imprinting was strong; Krek's "lovely Klawn" had followed, might still follow, to fulfill her and her mate's duty.

"I'll explore ahead. Any direction please you more than that one?" asked Lan, pointing into the setting sun.

"I feared you would say that because of the stream of running water being so close." The spider shivered and moved from Lan's side. "I even prefer the company of those in yon noisy caravan to the stream you are so desirous of crossing. The thought of water makes my legs tremble. The feeling of liquid running on them is indescribably horrid. It drips and mats the fur and—"

"A caravan?" Lan shinnied up a tree to peer

down into the valley at the sight Krek had seen long before him. A long trail of wagons curled like a brown segmented worm across the verdant green. Some were pulled by draft animals, while others puffed and chugged along, smokestacks pouring out clouds of steam from magically inspired engines. "People, Krek, people! And from the richness of their dress, this is a most prosperous world."

"Rich, perhaps, but soon to be deceased if aid is not immediately rendered them."

"What? I don't see anything."

"They are under attack," clacked Krek, his mandibles snapping together. "I see my first good meal in more weeks than I can remember." The bulky spider lumbered down the hill in full charge. Lan hesitated only a second before descending from the tree and following.

By the time they reached the bottom of the hill, Lan saw the caravan guards battling valiantly against dog-sized grasshopper creatures. But the droves of insects washed over them like an ocean's tide covering a beach. The bugs peered forth at their prey through compound eyes the size of Lan's fist. He knew the size exactly when he punched out to blind one intent on slashing off the arm of a woman in the nearest wagon.

"Are you all right?" he called to the woman. She turned a blanched face to him and silently nodded. Then he had no further time to worry about her safety. His own life hung in the balance.

Lan swung his sword and killed several of the grasshopper-things with each stroke, but sheer numbers soon tired him out. They swarmed, using their mandibles to nip tiny pieces from his sword blade, and he had to stay light on his feet to avoid their serrated legs. Every time he planted his feet to get a good swing with his sword, one buzzed past his guard and lashed out leg against leg.

Lan's boot tops soon flapped like so much ribbon about his ankles. The boots filled with blood oozing down his legs from half a hundred cuts. But he fought on, harder than ever before. The tide turned against the humans. Lan Martak saw the penalty for slacking his effort.

Judging by the partially devoured corpses on the ground, the insects had a taste for human flesh.

Lan was thrown to the ground by a tremendous explosion as one of the engine-powered wagons blew apart. One of the grasshoppers had crawled down the stack, causing pressure to mount. The Maxwell's demon inside had not ceased his selection of hot molecules; the steam continued to generate inside until the metal boiler walls suddenly gave way. Hot gas blasted across Lan's back, boiling hundreds of the insects.

It hardly made a dent in the voracious tide.

Krek proved the most effective fighter. He gobbled and gorged and fought with the ferocity of a hundred men. Somehow, this communicated to the grasshopper-things. Perhaps the spider was a potent natural enemy on this world, or they might have been intelligent enough to realize their potential meal dined off them. However it was, the grasshoppers began retreating with oversized froglike hind legs propelling them in immense ten-foot jumps.

"Come back, you dastards!" cried Krek around a mouthful of grasshopper, "I have not finished dining on you!"

Lan panted harshly as he leaned on his gore-encrusted sword. His legs wobbled under him, and his shoulders felt as if millions of heated needles were being thrust into his flesh. If the battle had continued another minute, he might have succumbed.

"Good fight, Krek. Looks like we turned the tide."

He saw the caravan master coming toward them. "We might be able to hire on as extra protection. At the very least, we can get a ride into the nearest town."

"Then we go to the cenotaph on the mountain?" asked the spider, finishing off the last tidbit of grasshopper.

"That, yes," said Lan. "We've got Inyx to find." Lan quietly added, "And Claybore to stop." They couldn't allow the sorcerer to conquer a world as lovely as this one. Together, they'd triumph against the mage.

Together, the three of them: Lan, Krek, and Inyx.

He turned to greet the wagon master.

"Are you certain your bandages aren't too tight?" asked Oliana n'Hes. She bent over in the creaking, rolling wagon to check Lan's fresh bindings.

"I'm fine, thanks," he protested, but the caravan master's wife's attentions weren't totally unwanted. Since he had saved her during the battle against the locusts, both she and her husband Huw had been solicitous of his health. Overly solicitous, Inyx might say.

Inyx.

The name burned bright in Lan's mind. Mentally he pictured the woman. Dark-haired, not beautiful but far from plain, she possessed a mental quickness and a physical prowess that were rare. She'd lost a husband and taken to walking the Cenotaph Road long before Lan Martak had discovered that route. Inyx battled and won, never compromising. She was her own woman, outspoken and direct.

Love? Lan didn't know if he loved her or not, but he felt more for her than simple comradeship.

Inyx would scoff at Oliana's attentions. If she'd been here.

"It's been almost a week. I've healed enough to be able to walk." Lan glanced outside the wagon bed and saw Krek lumbering along at an easy gait. The horses that hadn't been killed by the grasshoppers had been injured; they couldn't pull the wagons fast enough to make Krek do more than amble along. And the Maxwell's demon-powered wagons had fared even worse. Not a one of the mechanicals survived. Lan remembered the shrieks of joy as Huw had released the magically trapped demons into the world. They rocketed upward until vanishing in a low-hanging cloud layer.

It had rained continuously for the next three days.

"Without medicines or the proper spells, infection might set in."

"It hasn't yet," Lan gently pointed out.

"Don't go bothering the lad, Oliana," came Huw n'Hes's voice from the front of the wagon. "He needs sleep as much as anything else."

"I've gotten enough sleep this past week, thank you," replied Lan in exasperation. Being the conquering hero and the saviour of the wagon caravan had its drawbacks. "Do you mind if I join you, Huw?"

"Come ahead, lad."

Lan moved forward, acutely aware of Oliana's hot hand on his arm and hotter eyes, and sat beside Huw. The caravan master drove a rig now rather than riding ahead, because of the heavy toll taken by the insects. Not many humans had survived.

"Beautiful country," said Lan, his eyes drinking in the fresh green glory of the wooded landscape. "Reminds me of home."

"You walk the Cenotaph Road?" It came as a

question, but Lan sensed more of a statement in it.

"I do. My friend Krek and I became separated from a companion. We're looking for her. Is there any chance she might be in the city ahead, Melitarsus, I think you called it?" The name rolled off his tongue like a honey lozenge, rich and exotic. He felt his heart beat faster. Lan had wanted excitement, new worlds, and he now got it.

"Possible. It's the center for trade in this part of the continent. Oliana and I, we bring up barley and oats and *gurna* corn from the southlands. Melitarsus is a governmental seat, and its people can't be bothered with doing useful chores like growing food."

"You sound bitter about that."

"I make a good living out of supplying them what they don't have, but the taxes! A tax to get in, a tax to sell, a tax to leave. They've taxed everything but the taxes themselves."

"That's the function of any government. That's how they provide services, like these roads."

"These are toll roads. Privately owned. The Suzerain of Melitarsus uses the taxes for—"

"Now, Huw," came Oliana's sharp voice. "You mustn't discuss politics like that. Lan doesn't want to hear your opinions."

Lan did, but saw that nothing more was to be gained from pursuing the issue. Huw's conversation turned to his home in Lummin, overlooking Strange Point and the easternmost jut of the Sea of Wistry. The tone the man used told Lan that he preferred that part of the world to overcrowded, metropolitan Melitarsus.

Lan Martak's excitement mounted even more when he first sighted the gold-tipped spires rising at the corners of the walled city-state. Reflections from silver-capped sentries on the walls and the dark stream of wagons, both horse-drawn and magical, entering the gate opening at one side thrilled him. Above the ramparts circled long-winged aircraft, gliding on thermals, soaring, cruising, dipping downward to the earth. One of the flyers came so close to them that Lan caught a good look of his youthful face. The wind whipped sandy hair back from a wind-reddened face and tugged at a long white scarf around his neck. Then the flyer swooped, caught an updraft, and returned to his vigil above the city's walls.

Civilization again.

He'd been out on the road eating dust and drinking the odors of the animals too long. After all he'd been through, he longed for nothing less than a long, hot soak in a tub of scented water.

"Friend Lan Martak," came Krek's querulous voice. "Is *this* the place you want to be? Surely, you can choose better."

"Quiet, Krek. Melitarsus looks like my kind of place."

The spider only clacked his mandibles together in a deprecating fashion that Lan had learned to ignore. He was too happy at returning to civilization.

CHAPTER TWO

"I'll pay the entry fees for you and your friend," offered Huw. "And if you want to journey back to Lummin with Oliana and me, we'd consider it a rare privilege."

Lan heard the sincerity in the man's voice, but he saw more than friendship in Oliana's eyes. Such an arrangement could mean only trouble to him. The feeling of obligation wore off quickly, especially if Huw caught sight of Oliana's real interest in Lan.

"You're too kind to a stranger, Huw, but we must press on. We've got to find our companion."

"She must be very . . . special," said Oliana. She blinked slowly, her long dark lashes hiding her eyes in a sleepy-sexy manner. The careful circuit her tongue made around her ruby lips convinced Lan that he and Krek must be on their way soon—very soon.

"She is. I owe her much."

"Friend Lan Martak," called Krek. "Come look. They sell the bugs openly. Oh, this is such a *fine* place. I am glad I insisted we come." The giant spider had discovered a booth near the gateway leading into Melitarsus selling roasted insects. None was smaller than Lan's forearm, and many dwarfed even the giant grasshopper creatures they'd fought on the road. The spider bounced from one side to the other and, had he the capacity, would have drooled over the selection.

"I'd best take care of Krek," said Lan hurriedly. He shook Huw's hand and nodded to Oliana, not trusting the woman to any other platonic gesture.

"That you'd better. He's gathering quite a crowd."

Lan saw the caravan master spoke the truth. The owner of the concession stand cowered back against the stone wall of the city, his tiny charcoal burner untended. A large worm roasting over the coals no longer turned and began to burn.

"Here, allow me," said Lan, elbowing his way through the noisy crowd to aid the concessionaire. He began turning the worm to ensure an even cooking.

"He . . . he's with you?" asked the man, not taking his eyes off Krek.

"Yes. How much for the worm turning?" Lan indicated the one already spitted.

"Take it. Free. Just . . . move along. Please!"

"Free?" piped up Krek in a childlike voice. "My, my, this is a hospitable place. Thank you, friend." A dual clicking of his mandibles caused the worm to vanish. Lan replaced the skewer and slipped the booth owner a small gold piece. The denomination and mintage were of another world, but the metal retained its value across worlds.

As Lan and Krek worked their way from the booth, the spider commented, "I should have charged him for my services. His business has trebled since all saw the high quality of his new patron."

Lan Martak glanced over his shoulder and saw it was true. People thronged to the vendor begging for his wares. Lan shuddered at the thought of all the grubs being toasted and sold. He preferred his food less crunchy.

"Let's find a stable and arrange for a horse. That mountain is far enough away so that I don't want to walk to it."

"You need new boots, too, friend Lan Martak," observed the spider. "Those are doomed to an early demise."

The tattered fragments of leather remaining in Lan's boots convinced him that, while haste was necessary to find Inyx, he had to refit himself before any serious travelling. A horse, food, new clothes—boots!—and a sharpening of his sword and knife headed the list of items required. And he hadn't forgotten his vow to take a long, hot soak to ease the muscle strain he still suffered. In the past few weeks he had been through a lifetime of danger. His body required some attention now or it would fail him at a critical time in the future. Lan knew with innate certainty that finding Inyx would be a difficult task.

And combatting Claybore presented an even more difficult duty.

He tensed as he thought of the sorcerer, that eyeless skull, and even felt the tides of magic rippling around him in the city. Lan shook off the feeling of . . . compulsion. Few knew he had entered Melitarsus, and even fewer cared who he was. What magics he sensed were those already existing and weren't directed against him personally.

"This is a nice place. Streets swept, sanitation advanced, even a few of those things. I suspect Huw will purchase several to replace those he lost." Lan pointed to a chuffing, clanking, smoking wagon powered by steam. A Maxwell's demon sat trapped in the boiler, selecting hot molecules and keeping them while discarding the colder ones. "Those were becoming common on my world before I walked the Road. At least a dozen of them around town." When Krek only sniffed in disdain, he dropped the subject. He didn't bother telling the spider how he'd stolen one of the vehicles, promising the demon its freedom in exchange for a little distance between him and the law.

"I see fewer of the vendors selling succulent morsels," complained Krek. "I fear I might vanish unless I dine more frequently." Since he'd met the spider, Lan had noted a fullness developing around Krek's middle. He believed it came from overeating, but he said nothing. What thoughts went on inside that alien brain he had never figured out. Krek was a friend; Lan left it at that.

"There's a modest enough caravansary that will be adequate for my needs. I'm sure they can cater some bugs for you." Lan went into the inn, fascinated by the size of the place. While it didn't expand much on the ground, it rose to a dizzying height of four stories. Ordinary buildings weren't constructed like that on his home world. Only important edifices, like government buildings, or emperors' palaces, rose above the second story.

"Good day, gentle one," greeted the man behind a highly polished wooden bar. He leaned forward slightly, putting his weight on the bar. "Travelling from a distance?"

"Quite a distance."

"To?"

"I beg your pardon?" Lan's suspicions flared. What did it matter to this oily clerk where he travelled?

"I require it for the register." He pointed to a small book open in front of him. "The Suzerain requires it." He gave an eloquent shrug that indicated he was but a poor simple servant obeying the capricious whims of a bureaucrat. Lan made him out to be another bureaucrat revelling in paperwork.

"I don't know the name of the place."

"But you do know which direction you're travelling?"

"Toward the mountain," cut in Krek. "The big one. The one that is of a decent size on this otherwise flat world."

"The big one?" the clerk asked, puzzled. Then he brightened. "Mount Tartanius? You are pilgrims making the journey, then!"

"Yes," said Lan, not caring what journey the man referred to. All he wanted was a hot tub and time to rest in a soft bed.

"Affix your chop here," the clerk said, indicating a small portion of the page yet unfilled with his fussy writing. Lan obeyed, then hesitated. The clerk smiled and said, "That's all right. I'll enter the notation for your friend."

"He, uh, doesn't need a room," said Lan. "In the stables will be fine."

"A room," said the clerk firmly. "We wouldn't want to disturb the horses, would we?"

"No, we would not," agreed Krek.

The clerk beamed. Lan sighed. Being back in civilization had some compensations, but it also had drawbacks. He'd have to pay for two rooms to keep the spider from frightening the animals.

Lan Martak had just finished his second long bath of the day and felt almost human again when a hard knock came at his door.

"Who is it?" he called.

"Envoy from the Suzerain of Melitarsus," came the surprising answer.

"One minute," he said, getting into his trousers. He didn't bother with the ragged tunic or his ripped boots. If the envoy from the Suzerain of Melitarsus didn't like the way he dressed, that was just too bad. He had no reason to be rousted out like this. He hadn't even been in town long enough to violate any laws.

"Good day, gentle one," said the envoy, bowing in a courtly fashion.

"What do you want?"

"The Suzerain herself desires an audience with you."

"You mean she wants me to show up for an audience." The difference wasn't subtle. The envoy ordered him to the palace, or wherever the Suzerain kept her court.

"Not at all. Suzerain Nashira wishes to speak with you and your companion. At your convenience."

"You mean if I don't accompany you, I won't be forced along?" The shocked expression on the man's face told Lan much. This *was* a request, not an order. "Why does the ruler of Melitarsus want to see me?"

The envoy cleared his throat and nervously averted his eyes. Lan knew then what the answer would be.

"The, uh, spider. It . . . he . . . his like has never before been seen in Melitarsus. Smaller varieties, of course, abound, but none so large. The Suzerain wishes to observe him more closely."

"He's not a zoo beast," snapped Lan. Then, softening his tone, he said, "Krek's an intelligent being."

"Such is the appeal for Her Highness. She has heard reports of the encounter with the grub merchant."

"Any time I want, we can see the Suzerain Nashira?" asked Lan suspiciously.

"Not just any time, but certainly at your convenience, and if Her Highness is not caught by the press of official duties. She is a very busy woman."

"When would she like us to be there?"

"This evening?" the man suggested. "For a semi-formal dinner?"

"It'd have to be less formal than that. My clothes are a bit the worse for wear and tear."

"The Suzerain understands. Clothing suitable for the occasion will be sent. The third hour after sunset?"

"Fine," said Lan, puzzled. As he shut the door, he said to himself, "This is a more civilized city than I thought. Not only do I get a free meal, I get some clothes—and all for parading Krek around. Not bad, not bad at all!"

The tunic fit perfectly, but the gold threads cut into his flesh and the diamond bits woven into the fabric sent cold shivers throughout his body. Still and all, Lan Martak felt well taken care of. The envoy had chosen the clothing for him, and, while it didn't suit him as to taste, Lan had allowed the man to foist it off on him. This was the Suzerain's party.

Krek bounced from one side to the other in a nervous motion that soon got on Lan's nerves.

"Calm down, will you? They're not going to eat us for supper. The Suzerain herself invited us. She wants to meet you."

"Meet me? Me, a poor spider from the depths of the Egrii Mountains? On this world, there are not even any Egrii Mountains."

"You said you were a Webmaster. Doesn't that make you some sort of nobility?"

"Nobility?" shrilled the spider. "Far from it. I ran from my lovely Klawn after our mating. I forfeited my claim to any nobility with that cowardly act. I should have allowed her to devour me, to cocoon me for our hatchlings' first meal. What right have I to meet with nobility? My offspring may starve because of my failings."

Lan sighed and ignored the piteous whinings. He stared in frank admiration at the room in which they waited. The walls were frescoed by an artist of great talent. Every character seemed alive, eyes burning with emotion, their motion merely checked, the scenes intellectually involving and thrilling to study. On the floor lay a rug of a strong, fine weave that crushed delicately as Lan paced over it. As he walked, a tiny fragrance of pines rose to tease his nostrils. Gentle music reached his ears, music caused by his light steps on the rug; the combinations of feel, scent, and hearing beguiled him with the ingenuity. The furniture was on the sparse side and appeared too fragile for any significant weight; Lan decided against sitting in the antiques. The carved wood door had been polished to a luster approaching a mirror's, and the door lever might have been wrought from the finest of gold leaf. Lan couldn't wait to see the rest of the Suzerain's palace.

"This way, gentle ones," came the almost-whispered words of the chamberlain. He bowed as Lan and Krek passed him.

Lan hesitated as he passed. His arm had bumped into the chamberlain's. Cold metal instead of flesh ran under the lush velvet tunic. Seeing his reaction, the chamberlain smiled and said, "I am a mechanical. The human servants are reserved for more . . . personal duties."

"Totally mechanical?" asked Lan, frowning. The man—the mechanical—reached up and caught a corner of his face. He stripped back enough of the false flesh to reveal metallic bone.

"Totally mechanical," confirmed the chamberlain. "While it limits many things, it does relieve humans of tedious duties."

"I can imagine," said Lan, glancing back at the chamberlain. A slight clanking sound was the only indication that the servant wasn't completely human.

"By the Great Web," muttered Krek. "To spin a web here! It would be an act of daring and skill second to none."

The hall's vastness awed Lan. A four-story hotel had seemed extravagant use of time and material; it would fit into the chamber with space to spare on all sides. The vaulted ceiling of the hall vanished into the distance. He fancied tiny clouds formed their own weather patterns in the immense distance where the groined arch met. Pillars of alabaster supported the roof, and an opalescent material formed the floor. The entire audience chamber told of immense power and wealth—and, thought Lan, a rare quantity among rulers, great taste.

The pair clicked and walked along the floor to the far end of the chamber. At the raised throne sat a small child of indeterminate sex, hardly more than six or seven years of age. Lan's eyebrows rose at the idea of so young an urchin ruling Melitarsus.

"He's my son, gentle one," came a lilting voice

from Lan's right. He turned and again felt awe rising. The woman swirled past in a diaphanous gown that appeared to be spun of storm clouds and lightning, shifting, changing, rolling with vibrancy and power. The dark billows flowed in such a fashion that creamy skin was exposed as she moved; brilliant flashes of light were emitted from the deepest recesses of the fabric. A single strand of pearls circled the woman's throat. Other than this, she wore no jewelry.

"You are the Suzerain Nashira?"

"I am. And you are Lan Martak. And this is Krek of the Pinnacles, Krek-k'with-kritklik." How such an alien name flowed so easily from a human mouth amazed Lan. He'd tried for some time to properly pronounce Krek's name—and he'd repeatedly failed.

"Nashira," said Krek, bending all eight legs and forming a brownish lump in the middle of the gleaming opal floor. "You do this weak, pitiable one too much honor by your presence."

"Nonsense, it is Melitarsus that applauds you. I've heard of your exploits with the caravan, and your heroism. The least I could do was learn your name."

Lan frowned slightly. He couldn't pronounce Krek's full name, so how had Nashira learned it? Before he could pursue this line of thought, the woman spun about. Her dress opened slightly at the neckline from the motion and exposed a flare of lily-white breast that took Lan's mind off such erudition on the woman's part.

"Food. We must eat. Run along and play, Kyle."

"Do I have to, Mama? I want to watch the spider."

"Well, only if you behave." She smiled fondly as the child nodded, wide-eyed. "He's so good. He'll make a fine ruler for Melitarsus one day."

"You're so young, that day must be far in the

future," said Lan, trying for his most gracious of compliments.

"I'm older than I appear, gentle one, but thank you. Now, food. For all of us!"

Krek's mandibles clacked in a ferocious manner when he spied the delicacies prepared for him. An entire table had been laid with half the members of the insect kingdom.

"Your pardon, Suzerain," Krek said, his large dun-colored eyes focused on the platters presented for his approval. "I must honor you by doing justice to such fine food."

Nashira smiled as the spider began eating the grubs, worms, and insects fried, dipped, and spiced for him.

"Our other dishes are somewhat more enticing— to humans." She seemed unable to take her eyes off Krek, however, as she and Lan sat at a nearby table. Lan blinked hard as he "felt" magics surround him; the spells came from nowhere, seemed to be everywhere.

"This is a most progressive city, Suzerain," said Lan, trying to draw her attention away from Krek. "I noted you don't even use the royal 'we' when referring to yourself."

A dainty hand made a motion of dismissal.

"Such things are beneath me. Being Suzerain carries heavy burdens. My subjects, my loyal subjects, require continual work on my part. Taxes must be spent wisely."

"They seem to be," cut in Lan. "Melitarsus prospers."

"You like it here?" she asked, for the first time interested in him. Lan stirred uneasily. More than a faint touch of magic now flowed through the conversation. His magic-sensing ability "itched," but not enough to make him wary, just curious.

"The city is unparalleled in my travels. And it's ruler is the most gorgeous I've ever seen."

Nashira laughed lightly and said, "You flatter me. I'm not all that pretty. But beauty is in the eye of the beholder. If you name me lovely, then I must be."

Lan Martak basked in the warmth of her smile. While the woman was pretty, he had encountered lovelier ones. Zarella. Perhaps even Inyx. He felt a pang of regret. Staying in Melitarsus looked so attractive, but his duty lay elsewhere. Every day, every hour he delayed, might put Inyx into greater danger.

"Stay in our fair town and sample all we have to offer."

"The temptation is great, Suzerain—"

"Nashira," she corrected. "I don't stand on ceremony. We are very casual in Melitarsus."

"Nashira," he said. "But Krek and I seek a lost companion. We think she might be headed for Mount Tartanius."

"Mount Tartanius? She's a pilgrim, then?"

"No." Lan felt reluctance to tell even this charming woman of the Cenotaph Road and Claybore's existence, yet he must. But to ruin the mood . . .

"Oh," said Nashira, "then she must also walk the Cenotaph Road. There's been some activity atop Mount Tartanius that draws the pilgrims. They think a new road has been opened there now. It's a matter of faith with many of the cults that a cenotaph will provide the interworld travel they require from their religion."

"I've walked the Road," Lan said slowly. Nashira knew about the Cenotaph Road. Lan felt a surge of magic, then a slow fading, almost as if spells were being allowed to decay of their own accord.

"And followed adventure, you and Krek. Tell me, is the spider as mighty a fighter as he appears? He is frightful in the way he gobbles down those insects."

"He is stronger than any ten men, but he seldom fights."

"What?" Surprise, a hint of anger? "Why not?"

"He is a peaceful being. Like most spiders, he is more content to sit and wait rather than initiate."

"I see."

Nashira said nothing more, and silence fell. When Lan had eaten his fill and had begun to feel uncomfortable with the lull in conversation, he spoke.

"This has been a wonderful evening, Nashira. Thank you very much."

"Do come again tomorrow. For lunch. Yes, I'll be free of all my courtly duties by noon."

"We must ride on."

"To Mount Tartanius?"

"To find our companion."

"Well, Lan, this is difficult for me to say, but that wouldn't be wise." Seeing him tense, Nashira hurried on with her explanation. "The grasshoppers you defeated on your arrival to our world are swarming between here and the Sulliman Mountain Range. No two travellers are likely to survive the journey until fall chill brings a killing of the insects' food sources."

"We must try."

"Allow me to prepare an escort for you, then. An armed guard of company strength might win through."

"You are too kind."

"No, I just want you to agree to lunch tomorrow. Is that such a large price?"

Lan Martak felt magics flowing about him, but he couldn't decide if they were arcane or more secular. His silence lengthened uncomfortably.

"I insist," Nashira finally pressed. "One doesn't argue with the Suzerain of Melitarsus, does one?"

While Nashira's tone was light and joking, Lan felt a sharp bite to the words. No one ruled a city-state the size of Melitarsus without having at least an undercurrent of steel. Otherwise, a puppet sat on the throne while the real power resided elsewhere. Nashira ruled Melitarsus benevolently from all that Lan had seen, but she still ruled.

"Oh, yes, Lan, do accept Mama's offer," Kyle piped up. The child's wide-eyed innocence convinced Lan.

"Only until you have the troops assembled to guard Krek and me on our way to Mount Tartanius."

"You'll love this little place I've set aside for you," the woman continued. "You'll stay the night, of course." Her long, flowing dark hair caught the summer sun and sent back highlights of blue amid the black. In that moment, she reminded Lan a good deal of Inyx. Lan felt guilt at the thought of spending still another day in Melitarsus when he should be out seeking Inyx.

"I can only stay overnight. After lunch Krek and I must be on our way to Mount Tartanius. If the pilgrims can make it through the 'hoppers, then we can, also."

"Oh, Mama, look, look!" cried young Kyle. The boy pointed as Krek devoured the last of his meal. "See how hungry the spider is! None can stop him, none!"

"He is powerful. Look at the mandible action. Those can surely slash a man in half with one cut." The feral light in the lovely woman's eyes dimmed as she turned to Lan and said, "Your friend is needed here. He does the work of a dozen guards against the grasshoppers."

"Come, Lan, see the palace where Mama wants you to stay. I'm sure you'll like it." A tiny hand gripped his and pulled him along.

"Palace?"

"Kyle exaggerates. To him, anything larger than his quarters is a palace." The Suzerain trailed along behind, her billowing gown showing off her long, trim legs and the swell of her womanly breasts. Lan glanced behind him occasionally to drink in her beauty. She moved with such precision and grace that it was impossible to keep from staring. Nashira didn't mind; if anything, she basked in the attention.

"Here, Lan, isn't it marvelous?" The child stood and pointed.

"That's where you want me to stay?" Words choked in the man's throat. Kyle's estimation had been on the conservative side. This wasn't as much a palace as it was a small portion of Paradise. The neatly cropped lawns swept out for a mile behind. Trees dotted the landscape, and a small stream meandered across the meadows. The lushness of newly trimmed grass rose to bring back memories long buried in Lan's mind. Only in the distance did he see anything to spoil the illusion. The stone wall around the city-state gave the lie to limitlessness.

But the building itself shamed even the parklike qualities Lan admired so much. The walls were of finely wrought silver and gold; on closer examination he saw some artisan had spent considerable time creating scenes and stories. As he walked along the wall, a mural detailing the history of Melitarsus unrolled for his amusement. Some of the characters were bawdy, some sedate, all magnificently done.

"You like the outside, Lan? The inside is even nicer," cried Kyle. The boy pulled him along like a captive balloon.

"I don't believe this. It . . . it's magnificent." Lan's words barely touched what he felt. Everything about this building exceeded his wildest dreams. He took a deep breath; he'd possessed great wealth once before, and it had almost ruined him. The gold and jewels changed him, made him into something he wasn't. It required long practice to be wealthy without becoming arrogant. Nashira obviously had the practice; he didn't.

"I shouldn't," he said.

"But Lan, it's only for the night. You leave in the afternoon," she said, her words honeyed and enticing. "We wish to leave you with only good memories of the city."

"I have fine ones already. I know Krek dces. He is nearly bloated from dinner. But this!" Lan spun and studied the walls, the floor, the frescoed ceiling. The statuary of the finest marble, the busts of bronze, the oil paintings of extreme delicacy and craft, the very building itself was a masterwork. Ten mechanicals silently bowed, treating him as if he were the ruler of Melitarsus. He had the feeling all he had to do was snap his fingers and anything— anything at all—would be delivered to him.

"It's our guest house. Seldom is it used," said Nashira. "We reserve it for only the best."

"Like you!" chimed in Kyle.

"I'll stay. For the night."

"Good. You have these mechanicals. Simply call for them for anything you require. And there are human servants, also, if you prefer a more personal touch. Many guests are put off by being served by artificial beings." Her long, slender fingers lightly brushed his cheek. "But do enjoy yourself, Lan. Please." He felt both the erotic touch and the electric thrill of a magical spell. Then both Nashira and Kyle silently left.

"This is truly a sumptuous palace, friend Lan Martak," came the spider's familiar voice. "Have you seen my quarters? Marvelous! I've already begun spinning a sleeping web between the ivory posts. Most comfortable."

"Too comfortable," mused Lan, as he glanced around him. The place was more like a museum than a dwelling, yet Nashira had said it was a guest house. It hardly seemed plausible that an itinerate like himself merited such quarters, yet here he was. And there had been the flash of magic.

He shook his head. Perhaps the beauty of the room had been enhanced by simple magical spells. It wasn't unheard of. Perhaps no gold gleamed so brightly nor artist painted so brilliantly, unless aided by small magics.

It didn't matter. He'd enjoy himself. For the night.

CHAPTER THREE

"You're not drinking. Is anything wrong? Are you ill?" came the anxious words of the serving girl.

Lan looked at Ria and said, "How can I drink in the wine and your beauty at the same time?" She blushed nicely and turned to show him her profile. He'd tried to determine her age and had failed. Young, definitely, but a woman now. The ripeness of her breasts, the inviting width of her hips, the slim tapering of her graceful legs, all that indicated woman.

"Do you require anything further?" she asked. A strand of her red hair fell forward across her forehead. Quick, nimble fingers replaced the vagrant mane until her coiffure was again perfect. Dancing emerald eyes teased and hinted at pleasures no mere girl could know. It was Lan's turn to be confused.

"I'm stuffed. The food was excellent. I can barely finish this wine the Suzerain so kindly sent me."

"What a shame she is not here to share it with you." The way Ria said the words hinted at erotic worlds Lan only guessed existed. In a way it surprised him that the woman suggested that Nashira had any but passing interest in him.

"I'd rather . . ." Lan began, then stopped. His train of thought derailed as he "felt" powerful magical spells whirling around him. Then the sensation vanished.

"You'd rather be with me?" Ria asked innocently. But there was nothing innocent in the way she lithely rose to pirouette. As she turned, her garments began falling off in a teasingly erotic fashion. Lan got glimpses of snowy skin as her blouse sank down her back. When she turned, she held the blouse chastely over her breasts while her skirt seemed to have a mind of its own and creep up over the flare of her hips. A tiny puff of fiery red hair appeared before Ria spun around again, dropping the blouse to stand naked to the waist.

"I am not Nashira," she said slowly, "but I hope I can please you, nonetheless."

She turned and squarely faced Lan. He felt urges within his loins that hadn't stirred for some time. Fighting Waldron and Claybore had taken too much of his time and strength for the more pleasant activities life offered.

Ria offered the most pleasurable of all.

She came to him, her skirt slipping to the floor as she moved. By the time he took her in his arms, she was gloriously naked.

"Love me," she whispered hotly in his ear.

He rolled over to rise above her. Together their fingers removed his unwanted clothing. Then he made love to her, gently at first, then building needs until neither could stand another second. In a burst of fiery passion, they consummated their wanton desires.

Lan soon found himself responding to Ria's knowing ministrations anew.

"Look, my friends, behold how a barbarian makes love to a woman!" Nashira pointed to the wall of her immense audience chamber. The characters etched into the pounded gold mural began to writhe and move. The gold quality faded to be replaced by flesh tones. Soon, Lan and Ria moaned and strove ten times bigger than life in front of the crowd gathered before Nashira's throne.

"Lusty, isn't he?" came an effete voice from the Suzerain's right. "Hmm, interesting movement, that. Do you see how he turned her over so that she came up on hands and knees? Interesting technique, very interesting."

"Is that all it is to you, Clete? 'Interesting'?" taunted Nashira. "You make love like a mechanical. Why don't you show us what you've learned from Lan and demonstrate? On Aludra."

A honey blonde smiled and began stripping off already scanty clothes. The woman beckoned to Clete, who stood stock-still.

"Why don't you join me instead, Nashira?" the man asked. "All would enjoy that."

"Come, Clete, come and show me. Oh, look at what they do now. That is much more than *interesting*," said Aludra, her hands working down the front of the man's tunic, around his waist to cup firm buttocks. Then she slipped her fingers lightly around to his codpiece. "Not all of this is cotton padding," she said, her voice now husky.

All the while, Nashira watched Clete and Aludra— and the others—slowly working themselves up into erotic frenzy. A full five hundred of her nobles had turned out for sport this evening. The attraction was obvious. Few visitors to Melitarsus showed the energy that Lan did. Nashira smiled and leaned back in her throne, her long, slim legs unconsciously spreading as she watched the pair magically shown on the wall. She reached out and silently took a cup of aphrodisiac-laced wine from an expressionless mechanical waiter.

"Ah, yes, Lan Martak and my little Ria, you are quite an attraction," sighed the Suzerain of Melitarsus, sipping at the cinnamon wine. She felt a stirring of her long skirts and glanced down. A small lump worked its way upward. She felt hot breath along her naked legs, and shivered in anticipation. Her eyes returned to the screen as her own passions rose, were fed, were tended. She shrieked out her joys, then relaxed.

She blinked rapidly to clear her vision. Aludra and Clete had long since split up. Aludra and two other women were intimately engaged, while Clete and another woman were slowly warming to one another. All had their eyes fixed on the wall, however. Orgies became so dull after a while. It required a special attraction to add zest to them. The magical eye spying on Lan certainly gave her nobles new life this night, thought Nashira.

The roar of passion rose from the five hundred—or more—gathered in the audience chamber. She barely heard the child's voice over the groans and gasps.

"Can I go now, Mama? Will there by anything else?"

"No, Kyle, run along."

The child licked his lips, smiled, and vanished like a ghost. Nashira smoothed her skirts, closed her eyes, let her hand roam her lush body, and lost herself once again to her own sexual needs.

*   *   *

"You look disconsolate this fine morning, Krek. Is there anything I can do?" asked Nashira. She turned to face the giant spider, her skirts floating out from around her slender legs like a pale green nimbus. Sparks darted throughout the fabric, giving the dress the look of a sea caught on fire.

"Nothing," said Krek, munching on an especially large grasshopper he'd caught invading the premises.

"Surely, you cannot be wanting for food?"

"No."

"Come, now," said Nashira, her hands stroking over the coppery bristle of the spider's nearest leg. "Tell me. I want only to help."

"Very well." The spider twitched his body around and started off. Nashira kept her hand on the spider's leg as they went into the lavish quarters the Suzerain had given Lan. "Listen" was all Krek said.

Nashira's lips turned upward in a wicked smile. The unmistakable sounds of Ria and Lan together echoed throughout the building. She felt herself becoming excited as she eavesdropped. While not so potent a stimulus for her as using the magic eye, this nevertheless provided her imagination with vistas hitherto untapped. Her hand tightened on Krek's furry leg, and she began stroking up and down more vigorously.

"It has been like that all night long. He and that red-headed servant have been performing your silly human mating rituals. No, he cannot find the energy to leave this morning for our trip to Mount Tartanius. He is too tired to leave bed—and so is she, one would think."

"What's one more day in our fair city?" asked Nashira, moving closer to the spider. Her legs parted slightly, and she thrust herself against the thick, furry appendage. "Aren't we treating *you* right?"

"Quite so, Nashira. For that I thank you. But you are treating that weak human friend of mine *too* well. We might never leave."

"Would that be so odious? Melitarsus is a place where all things can happen, all good things."

Krek looked at her, as if for the first time. He twitched his leg and pulled it from her grasp.

"I feel dampness on my leg. You sweat, perhaps."

"Let's go exploring in the city and see if we can't find something to keep you amused." Nashira pulled away from Krek with some reluctance and smoothed her skirts.

"If I enjoy myself one-half as much as he," Krek said, bobbing his head toward the archway leading to Lan's sleeping quarters, "I might not want to leave, either."

"I'd like that," said Nashira earnestly. "In fact, this very day is an occurrence you will be sure to enjoy."

"I am your humble servant." Krek performed an awkward bow that made Nashira smile even more broadly. She held out her hand and Krek placed one chitinous claw lightly in it. Together, spider and Suzerain left, the passionate sounds soon behind them.

"There are certainly enough people gathered about," observed Krek. "But why? We seem to be the center of attention." The spider stood in the center of a sand-covered arena, walls rising up all around before the banks of seats curved back. Not an empty chair was to be seen.

"They have come to see your fighting prowess."

"Fight? Me? I do not fight."

"Not even for me, O Mighty Krek?" asked Nashira, her hand softly rustling the copper-colored bristles on his leg.

"Why fight? There is no need. Such things are peculiarly and tediously human. We spiders might seem bloodthirsty, but such is not the case. In fact, we . . ."

The three men entering the arena were naked to the waist, their bare, muscular bodies gleaming with lubricants. They parted as they came from a single gateway on the far side of the pit, then drew long swords. The silvery sheen reflected back to the spider.

"What is this?" he demanded of Nashira.

"If you do not defend me, they will have their way with me."

"So?"

"They will then kill me. And you." The woman's voice became husky, passionate. "You must fight, Krek. You must kill them. *Do it!*"

The men attacked in a precision movement. The one on the left flank drew Krek's attention while the one on the right moved in for the kill. The one in the center poised on the balls of his feet to jump in either direction to aid whichever of his comrades required it.

A powerful overhead slash would have ended Krek's life if the spider hadn't gathered all eight legs under him and jumped straight up. The sword buried itself in the ground—and Krek's descending body weight buried his would-be killer. Hard claws pinned the man down.

"Get him!" cried Nashira. The remaining two swordsmen were already on the attack. They circled and came at Krek from opposite sides. The spider shivered as if he had a palsy. As the men attacked, two of Krek's long legs shot out, catching them both in the midriff. They stumbled backward, swords and attack forgotten. One landed heavily, the wind knocked out of him. The other turned and ran.

"Why do they wish to harm me?" asked Krek in a small voice. "I have done nothing to them."

"Fight, damn you!" screamed Nashira. ."Don't let that one get away."

"You wish me to stop him? Oh."

The spider made a coughing sound, then a gurgling came from deep inside. A spinneret opened on his abdomen and a long, silken strand rocketed forth. The strand arched across the arena and dropped on the fleeing man's back. A long, agonized scream sounded as Krek reeled him in. He fought in vain against the silk rope now encircling his body.

"Here, Nashira," said Krek.

"Look. Three more!" cried the Suzerain. She backed away until she felt the firmness of wooden wall behind her. The woman picked up a fallen sword and thrust it into the sand in front of her. "Kill them, Krek. Defend me! Defend yourself!"

"I do not understand why they attack," said the spider, bemused. A humming noise filled the arena as more and more of the sticky strands of webstuff shot forth to entangle his opponents' legs. But the number of men entering the pit soon exceeded Krek's ability to produce web.

A quick slash of his mandibles cut one man in half. Fountains of blood gushed onto the dry sand, to be quickly sucked up. The crowd went beserk, cheering and screaming.

"Yes, Krek, that's it! Do it! Kill them! Kill them all!" Nashira stepped forward, lifting her skirts. The pommel of the buried sword rested cool and round between her thighs, but her eyes never left the carnage in front of her. Krek bounced from side to side, appearing awkward in his movement but giving death to any who came within his range. One mighty snap of his pincers broke a finely

tempered steel sword flailing too close to his head.
Again the crowd left out a frantic cheer.

Nashira bobbed up and down, moaning, sobbing,
urging on the spider in his battle against a full
dozen armed and armored men.

Krek glanced at the woman, saw the look of
stark ecstasy on her face, and didn't understand.
Even less he understood the reason for these men
trying to slay him. They fought with single-minded
determination, yet he had never before seen them.
They weren't his enemies. They weren't the grey-
clad soldiers who had invaded his world and many
others along the Cenotaph Road. Most of all, they
weren't being sent by Claybore to permanently
remove him.

The spider considered the question, then decided
to be vexed.

He fought without hesitation now, his potent
death scythes snapping and clacking, closing on
human arms and legs and torsos. One quick nip
severed a man's head from his body. A geyser of
blood ten feet high shot aloft. The crowd went
berserk.

"Nashira, what is happening?" demanded Krek
during a brief respite from the battle. Fourteen lay
dead and mutilated in front of him while another
seven limped back to the gateway at the far side of
the arena. The Suzerain of Melitarsus let out a tiny
gasp, then shook all over like a leaf in a high wind.

When she stepped away, the sword was still
buried in the sand, the pommel damp and shiny
with her juices.

"Krek, you fight like a juggernaut. You are superb! Can you fight any more?"

"Why? Why are they attacking me? I have done
nothing to them."

"For a gourmet feast of insects. Succulent bugs,

the finest in all of Melitarsus. Will you kill again for that, Krek?" she cried.

"I have worked up a hunger," admitted the spider, "but why must I slay these poor, fragile humans?"

"There. They come again!" Nashira cried. She pointed. A wedge of ten soldiers armed with pikes advanced on the spider.

Krek leaped into the air, all eight legs acting like coiled springs. But the soldiers reacted swiftly, their pikes planted in the sand, deadly barbed points aimed aloft. A collective gasp came from the throats of everyone in the audience. The spider now met his fate.

Krek saw the ten pikeheads turn upward. In the same instant, he spit forth a long strand of web-stuff. It arrowed upward and clung tenaciously to a thick beam overhead supporting part of the arena bleachers. The spider swung, his body passing just inches above the pikes. His clawed feet raked across the massed men, killing six. As he swung back, he shortened the strand and avoided the thrusting pikes of the remaining men who had thought to skewer him.

Krek cut loose from the strand of web and dropped. The soldiers fought, but with so many of their friends dead, they fought in disarray. Krek backed them against a wall, then attacked. His mandibles closed on metal; he fought mechanicals now. One long, hard slash ripped the artifical skin from the face of one, exposed the metallic legs of another. These soldiers did not bleed and die, but they proved easier to disable. They fought because they'd been ordered to, but lacked the human re-serve to keep fighting, no matter the odds.

Krek disabled the mechanicals one piece at a time, until only twitching, thrashing parts remained. The crowd cheered wildly and began throwing flowers. Krek bent and sampled one of the tastier-looking ones. It had only bland appeal, nothing like a juicy grub or worm. He returned to find Nashira propped against the wooden wall.

"Nashira, are you injured?" asked the spider, concern in his voice. "The front of your dress shows—"

"I am fine, Krek. You are magnificent!" She ran to him and hugged a gory leg. "They love you. *I* love you."

"Why, thank you. But this killing. I don't understand it. Humans do peculiar things, but this is totally senseless. I do not like being set upon by those mechanical servants, either. Their parts nick my mandibles." He tentatively clacked his pincers together, listening to the sound they made.

"Smell the blood, Krek. Doesn't it heighten your senses, all your senses?" she cooed.

"Smell? I have argued this point with Lan Martak. His claims for this purported sense are too wild to believe. Taste is adequate."

"Ah, you want insects. Insects you shall have!" Nashira clapped her hands and servants came forth bearing silver serving trays laden with insects of every description, small ones, large ones, prepared in a dozen different fashions. "Enjoy yourself, Krek. You've earned it."

The spider looked around the arena. Men with litters removed the dead and dying. A funny tremor rose inside. He felt awful about the killing, but before he could put voice to it, Nashira's soft voice reached him. The chant was lyrical, enticing. He became engrossed in the intricate patterns of sound. When the Suzerain of Nashira had finished her geas, Krek found himself totally unable to say a single word about the slaughter.

He shrugged, a rippling, sinuous motion, then

began his feast. He disliked the killing, but the bugs were definitely to his taste.

Nashira watched, smiled, anticipated even more to come.

CHAPTER FOUR

Lan Martak rolled over, stretched, yawned, then stretched some more until all his muscles felt taut and ready for action. But that was the problem. There wasn't any action. Everything in his life was perfect. He lived in the most sumptuous of mansions, a dwelling beyond his wildest dreamings. He had the richest, tastiest of foods to eat and the finest of clothes to wear. There were no demands placed upon him. The Suzerain of Melitarsus saw him but seldom, requested his presence even less. The only real demand was of a pleasurable kind.

Ria was sexually insatiable. She knew tricks that Lan had never even heard of, much less tried, and she was wantonly willing to demonstrate anything and everything for him.

"Dammit!" he cried out. "I'm bored!" He felt like he'd gotten trapped in a cage. Guilt worked on him, too, knowing that Inyx wandered the Cenotaph Road alone. The only consolation Lan found lay in the fact that Inyx was independent and able to take care of herself. Yet he blamed himself for not making a more determined effort to leave Melitarsus and all the creature comforts, to brave the deadly grasshopper infestation, to climb the precipitously tall Mount Tartanius and find the cenotaph and possibly Inyx.

He heaved a deep sigh, then scratched himself.

"Claybore," he muttered to himself. "The grey-clad soldiers will swarm over this world. Claybore will rule along the entire Cenotaph Road unless I warn people about him, try to stop him before the conquest proceeds too far." Lan worried over this. Many times he'd tried to broach the subject with Nashira, and had found the words jumbling in his throat. It was as if he couldn't tell her anything that might alarm her. Yet he had to keep trying. Nashira, indeed, all in Melitarsus, had to be warned of the danger posed by the decapitated sorcerer.

He didn't know the true extent of Claybore's territorial expansion. One world? A hundred? He had hints that the sorcerer had just begun when he encountered Waldron on the bleak world, but those remained hints, not facts. Nashira seemed to know of the grey-clads but felt no anxiety about their presence. The little scouting beyond the confines of his gossamer prison Lan had done showed no evidence of Claybore's men, but the adventurer would be the first to acknowledge he had not made any comprehensive check.

The entire city-state of Melitarsus might be overrun with them and he wouldn't know it.

"Hello, friend Lan Martak," came the doleful greeting from the direction of the doorway. Lan looked up but saw no one.

"Come on in, Krek."

"It is all right? You and that red-furred serving woman are not mating?"

"She doesn't have red fur. That's hair. And no, we're not mating."

The spider bounced into view, filling the arched doorway. On either side of the arachnid, buried as decoration in the walls, gleamed jewels Lan took for diamonds. The spider appeared to wear them as a necklace as he bent to enter.

"You perform such feats constantly."

"Hardly feats," said Lan, then he laughed. "Maybe they are, with Ria. She's an agile one."

"Almost as agile as a spider."

Lan looked more carefully at his friend. While the spider's grooming had never been more immaculate or his belly more filled with tasty bugs, Krek's attitude struck a discordant note. Seeing him despondent was nothing new; having their moods match so closely worried Lan.

"What's wrong, old spider?" he asked. "You're mighty morose."

"I . . ." the spider began, then stopped, making a choking noise. Lan sat up, concerned. Not only had he never heard Krek cough like this before, he felt the gentle winds of magic wafting through the chamber. Lan tried to put some name to the spell and failed. His abilities in casting spells were limited to a few healing chants and a pyromancy lore for starting fires. At detecting spells he had more facility, but this one eluded him. It almost fit into a pattern, almost became describable, then it faded away and left him, like the miasma of a subtle perfume.

"They're grooming you well enough. I don't remember ever seeing your fur shine like it does now."

"My legs are rather well tended, are they not? And my abdomen has never been more nicely polished."

"Food? They're giving you all the right kinds of insects?"

"Oh, superb insects!" cried the spider, showing some signs of enthusiasm on the subject. "Even my quarters are everything one of my persuasion might require. Mechanicals clean it properly, doing my exact bidding. I have spun a new and more intricate web every day this week. It is only that . . ."

"That you think we should be moving on, working to find Inyx?" Lan rushed the words out to make sure he actually voiced them. He felt a strange reluctance to speak of such matters, just as he did of telling Nashira about the menace posed by Claybore.

"Yes!"

Krek's vehemence startled him.

"Nashira promised an escort."

"She has not provided it."

"Her troops are all occupied fighting the 'hoppers. We can't ask her to free up some of them just to escort us on our way. Saving the lives of her people in outlying areas is more important."

"What outlying areas?"

"The ones outside the walls. She said her men are on constant guard outside."

"The entire of Melitarsus is within the walls," said the spider.

"What are you trying to say, Krek? That Nashira lied to me?"

"I . . . I must go, friend Lan Martak."

"Krek, wait a minute. This is serious." But the spider bobbed about, turned, and ducked through the doorway before Lan could stop him. The man got to his feet and started to follow. He ran into Ria before he got outside the building.

"Lan," she said in a husky, suggestive voice. "You come looking for me."

"No, I wanted Krek. He—"

"This isn't for me?" she whispered, her hand working down over his naked belly, then slipping even lower. Even though he began to physically respond, Lan's mind remained apart. Apart and worried. Something was wrong.

And he didn't know how that could be when everything was so right.

* * *

"Fifty on the spider!" came the cry.

"Covered. Give me odds."

"Three to one!"

The betting went on as Krek stood in the middle of the arena, outwardly placid. Inside, his spiderish emotions churned. He killed through necessity, not for sport. Arachnids were mighty hunters, vicious opponents, but not wanton killers. Yet he had become that. Every day he came to the arena, stood in the sandy pit, and sent dozens of men and women to their deaths not because of physical hunger on his part, but because of psychic hunger on the part of the spectators.

In a way, killing the mechanicals was even worse. They did not bleed, but their expressionless faces haunted him. Powered by some technology he didn't understand, the mechanicals obeyed and perished as surely as if they were flesh and blood.

He tried to stop himself and failed each time. While no mage, his abilities to deal with magic were more pronounced than Lan Martak's. Krek felt the spells used on him but couldn't sidestep them. The more he tried to fight them, the more potent they became.

Nashira, Suzerain of Melitarsus, proved herself a powerful mage.

Krek turned and studied the woman indolently reclining in the royal box perched on the edge of the wall. She smiled at him, took a sip from a drink laced with aphrodisiac, then slowly nodded her head. Gates opened and men trotted out, armed men intent on killing. Nashira flicked her hand and a score of human serving girls hurried to her side. They stripped her naked, then began sensuously applying oils as their nude sovereign watched the beginning slaughter in the arena.

"Kill!" shrieked the nearest man.

Krek's mandibles severed the swordsman's arm. He died amid a spray of his own blood.

"Circle," came the more cautious command from the senior of the remaining soldiers. "I've watched previous bouts. He's big, he's strong, but we can bring him down."

Krek lightly jumped a flung net, cut a pike's head off, kicked out and buried a hardened claw into the midsection of a careless mechanical. The actions came automatically now. He tried not to think of the suffering he caused or the intense emotion of those watching.

He tried not to think of the intense emotion welling inside himself. The spider's delicate sensibilities twisted and soured at this slaughter; the men never presented a different attack.

In spite of himself, he turned to study Nashira. The woman moaned softly now, her eyes half-hooded and her body arching so that her servants could rub the pungent oils over every square inch of skin possible. The spider couldn't decide if the bloody slaughter or the erotic touches aroused Nashira most. It might have even been a combination, one no good without the other.

"Stop, please," he begged as the soldiers advanced. "I do not wish to slay you. I am more powerful, more skilled. Leave me alone!" The shrill wailing cut through the roar of the crowd and caused a hush to fall. The men facing Krek shifted uneasily from foot to foot, wondering how to react.

"It's a trick," said one of the men. "He's done this before. He lulls us into a false sense of security, then attacks."

"You're sure about that, Neeck? He sounded sincere."

Neeck laughed harshly. "My best friend, Lor n'Histima, thought he sounded sincere, too. Lor's dead these past four days, him and four mechs. That bug bloody ripped his head off!"

Krek heard the exchange as if from a distance. Nashira's moans and softly muttered words rang like bells in his head. The spell she cast worked on him, drove him insane with bloodlust, brought out the most vicious of his arachnid hunting instincts.

Unable to stop himself, Krek lunged. Four men died in a single slash of his pincers. Four of his legs drove forth, buried deep in unarmored chests. He recovered, bounced as if on springs, then shot forth a sticky hunting web. The elastic band rocketed out, curled around the body of the remaining soldier, then slowly pulled the struggling man inward. Krek's insides twisted when he saw the raw fear on the face, felt the shaking of stark panic, saw the voiding of the man's bowels.

A single snip removed the man's head. The body shook and escaped in one direction while the look of fear on the man's face became a permanent feature in death. The head lay ten feet away in the sand.

The crowd went beserk. Cheers echoed throughout the city and gamblers collected bets.

Inside his head, Krek heard Nashira's voice say, "You have done well, spider. Your servants will clean you, tend to your needs. You are the champion of all Melitarsus." Mocking laughter faded and left Krek alone and weary in his own skull.

He tried to form the words, to practice them so that he could tell Lan Martak what happened to him every day. Only inarticulate gurglings emerged. Tears of frustration formed in the spider's eyes as mechanical attendants led him from the arena.

"How are you today, Kyle?" asked Lan Martak of the Suzerain's young son. The boy looked up at him, eyes wide. For no reason, Lan felt a shiver of dread up and down his spine.

"I am fine, thank you," came the polite reply. "You are very good."

"Beg pardon?" asked Lan, surprised. "Good at what?"

Kyle's lips pulled back in a grin that hardly belonged on a seven-year-old face. The laughter accompanying it bordered on the demented.

"My mother will see you now, if you like," said the boy, his mood shifting swiftly. The brief view of something demonic passed. Only innocent child remained.

"Thank you," said Lan uneasily. He walked the length of the audience chamber, conscious of the rumbling echoes his bootsteps made and feeling all the more anxious because of it. He might have been a soldier called before his commanding officer rather than an honored guest seeking out his hostess.

"Lan, it's been so long since we've talked," greeted Nashira. She rose, her arms outstretched to him. He allowed himself to be hugged, scenting the gentle essences of her perfume and brushing his cheek against her lustrous blue-black hair.

"It's over a week," he said.

"Too long. Do forgive me. Matters relating to the city have been taking too much of my time. Those damned 'hoppers," she said, sadly shaking her head. "They grow worse rather than better. I fear we'll have to resort to sterner measures."

"Magic?" he suggested. Lan felt the woman tense slightly. She recovered quickly and shook her head. "Not that. The people of Melitarsus would never stand for it."

"Why not?"

"As useful as magic can be, they've had bad experiences. My grandfather overthrew a sorcerer to gain the throne. The sorcerer had misused his power and enslaved the populace, making them no more than his personal servants. My grandfather vowed that no Suzerain of Melitarsus would ever again practice magic—or allow its practice within the walls. We have our mechanicals to serve us and do not need spells. The wagons powered by demons are imported and not allowed to remain longer than a week, and our flyers are totally wind-powered, no magics at all used."

"But you're a sorcerer," blurted Lan, regretting the words immediately.

"What do you mean?" Sharp, hard.

He covered, saying, "Your beauty ensorcells me. Your intelligence enthralls me. Your wisdom transcends magic."

Nashira laughed delightedly.

"You're such a rogue, Lan. I'm so happy you have come to Melitarsus. None of my court say such things to me. Not a one. All my ministers talk of is crops and cash flow, road repair and how to fend off the next wave of 'hoppers. They are *so* dull." Her long fingers stroked over his cheek, the dark-painted nails cutting slightly into his flesh to leave small red crescents. Lan felt an electric tingle pass throughout his body, do things to him.

His magic sense screamed.

"I hate to burden you with further demands on the city's resources, but Krek and I really must press on. What is the chance of getting the escort you promised?"

"Escort?" she said, swirling away. Her dress shifted colors like a rainbow. A flawless naked back turned to Lan. She studied him from over her shoulder. The man wondered how the dress stayed pressed so intimately to the front of her body when there was no support behind.

"Soldiers. To escort us to Mount Tartanius."

"Oh, yes, those men," she said. As she moved, the colors of her dress changed from bright oranges and reds to more sedate greens. Wedges of black formed and powered through the pastels, replacing them totally. It was as if the dress altered with her mood. Even as he watched, colors flowed into new hues, took on different configurations, some patches of the dress even becoming transparent. Lan almost choked when strategic portions of the dress turned clear, but the clarity of the view of Nashira's most intimate parts clouded, turned opaque, and began shifting through an artist's palette of colors.

Lan shook himself. The sensation of being trapped threatened to panic him.

"The hospitality you've shown is second to none," he heard himself say, almost as if another spoke. The feeling of distance within himself grew. Panic mounted. Magics flared brightly all around him. He tried to warn her of Claybore. All he uttered was, "I can't fault you on even the smallest of points."

"Then stay!" she cried. "Stay in Melitarsus. We need more men like you."

"I do nothing," he protested. "That's the problem. I . . . I do nothing at all."

"I can make you a lord of the city. Your fighting prowess is obvious. How would you like to be deputy commander of the watch? It carries both prestige and great duty. You would be second in command of the army, next only to General Clete n'Fiv."

"No, Nashira, please."

"I can't make you commander. That wouldn't be the least fair to Clete."

"I'm not asking for that. I just want to continue on to Mount Tartanius."

"You're no pilgrim. What's there you can't find

in Melitarsus? Some woman? If Ria displeases you, select another!"

Lan Martak felt a surge of cold insight. If he expressed desire for Nashira, that meant his death, yet the woman used sexual charms on him, teasing and taunting. Even as she spoke, portions of her dress became crystal clear again, portions showing the furry nest between her thighs, the pink-capped mounds of her breasts. The sexual message clearly served as an inducement to stay, yet the ruler of Melitarsus remained aloof, untouched, untouchable. She would give him anything to keep him, anything but herself.

The contradiction confused him.

"The escort. Do we get it?"

"Oh, Lan, you are so stubborn. Be on your way. But let the spider remain, if he so chooses."

This took Lan by surprise. It had been Krek who had given him the impetus to come and confront Nashira. The woman's tone told him that she fully expected Krek to remain behind if he decided to push on to the mountains. He couldn't think of a single thing that bound Krek to this city, to this woman. The spider preferred the mountains where he could range as he had as a hatchling, as a Webmaster. Melitarsus offered nothing but a tiny room in which to spin his webs.

"He'd come with me."

"Why not let Krek decide for himself?"

Nashira sounded too sure of herself for Lan to debate the issue.

"You have no qualms about letting us leave, if we both choose to do so?"

"Of course I do!" she protested. "The 'hoppers are deadly this year. Your devoured carcasses would be found by the side of the road come fall. I like you—both of you. That's the last thing I'd want. Stay, Lan, stay here. Enjoy all Melitarsus has to offer, at least until the autumn chill kills off the grasshoppers."

Lan Martak sensed magic building all around him. The audience chamber wavered slightly. He saw Nashira as if through a heat shimmer. His senses jumbled, reminding him of the instant/eternity he'd spent in the white foggy limbo between worlds. The colors of the woman's dress blazed brilliantly now; her pungent perfumes made his nostrils flare; oceans roared in his ears. He felt a power growing within him, growing from a tiny seed within his mind, turning into something stronger, more vibrant, more commanding.

"Kyle!" the woman said sharply.

Lan felt the magical power used against him slacken. He almost fell to his knees when it vanished entirely. Pale and shaken, he stood before Nashira. The expression on her face combined anger and pride. Peering out from around her skirts like a much younger child stood Kyle.

"You appear faint, Lan. It's nothing I said, is it?"

"What?" He slowly recovered. His senses returned to normal, and the compelling flow of magic around him ebbed. "Sorry, my mind wandered elsewhere."

"That is sometimes dangerous. If your mind wanders, you might be tempted to join it."

Lan said nothing.

"Go, my good friend, relax in your quarters. Take a soothing bath. Tell Ria I've ordered the physician to send you some medicine. You'll be hale and hearty before you know it."

"All should be cared for as Krek and I are," said Lan, bowing slightly.

"All should be as stimulating as you and the spider are," said Nashira. Her laughter followed him out of the audience hall.

*   *   *

Lan Martak ducked down an alley, fear clutching at his throat. He didn't think they'd seen him. If they had, a half-dozen swords would have been sheathed in his body by now.

He'd left Nashira's palace, distraught by all that had occurred. The visit hadn't produced the hoped-for results. She had given him no promise of troops to escort him and Krek through the 'hopper infestation; Nashira had promised more than any mortal could hope for in a lifetime. All the parts of this puzzle failed to come together. If Krek were right and the Suzerain maintained no army outside the walls of the city-state, she could supply a score of troops—more!—without diminishing her defense capabilities.

That didn't fit, nor did the surge of magic he'd felt just before leaving her presence. The woman lied when she said that magics weren't used by the rulers of Melitarsus; he'd felt ephemeral spells inside the chamber from the very first audience. No spell, however, had been so strongly antagonistic as the last one.

And he didn't think Nashira had been responsible for it.

But Kyle? Lan tried to remember what mages he'd known had said about magic. That it required long years of study he knew. Never had he heard of a sorcerer as young as Kyle. Even native ability had to be trained over decades.

He'd wandered the streets of Melitarsus pondering all this when he'd bumped into a grey-clad soldier.

Only quick reaction had allowed him to twist into the alley and run for his life. The pounding of feet behind him told Lan all he needed to know. The startled soldier had only caught a brief glimpse of him, but he knew Lan. The way he called out to his companions proved that beyond any possible doubt.

Claybore still wanted him, still had men tracking him.

Finally eluding the grey-clad soldiers hadn't been easy, but he knew the city better than they. Panting, heart racing, he leaned against the city wall and observed.

While the number of the grey soldiers inside Melitarsus wasn't large, it was obvious these were scouts. Before the end of the summer the city would be overrun with them. Melitarsus would fall, just as a hundred other cities had. Lan remembered how they'd insinuated themselves into his hometown, how Kyn-Allyk-Surepta had turned traitor, sold out to them, become a ranking officer.

They started innocuously, offering their services to beleaguered law enforcement agencies. Lan didn't doubt for an instant that the grey-clad soldiers were behind the increases in crime that they claimed to abhor and oppose. As the populace depended more and more on the interlopers and less on their own officials, the grey soldiers' grip tightened. Soon enough, they were the only authority, and any speaking out against them mysteriously died.

When their power became complete, the disappearances were no longer mysterious. They became public executions.

Zarella had died mysteriously, and Lan Martak had been accused of her murder—by Surepta.

The pattern repeated in Melitarsus. The minor variations mattered little.

Lan hurried on when he saw another tiny knot of the soldiers advancing. They laughed and joked among themselves, but their eyes were alert. They sought him. Whether or not Claybore directed them, the grey-clads were a menace and one that Lan couldn't ignore. Little good Nashira's protection if they killed him in the street.

He went into a pub and sat with his back to a wall, face down. The soldiers entered behind him. Lan tensed, his fingers gripping tightly on the hilt of his knife. He calculated how to kill the leader, then work on to the others while confusion still held them. It wasn't necessary. They talked briefly with the innkeeper, then were summoned by a woman who had remained outside. Lan didn't get a good look at her, but she wore the grey uniform.

The man finally approached Lan, after watching the soldiers leave.

"What'll ye have, eh?"

"Ale and some information."

"Might be able to get ye both," he said suspiciously. His expression relaxed when Lan dropped a pair of gold coins on the table.

"The soldiers. What do you know of them?"

"Those boys?" the man laughed. "Ye fear them? No need. They only help out. Been havin' trouble with both some young vandals and those damn 'hoppers. Since them greys showed up, no trouble with neither. Right good fellows, they are. Even a woman commandin', too. Damn unusual in these parts to see that, but she's an honorable one. They do good keepin' the disruptive elements out. Now, what kind of ale can I do for ye?"

"Never mind," said Lan. He left the coins. He left the pub. The pattern repeated. The subjugation of Melitarsus had begun.

CHAPTER FIVE

"Turn this way, Lan my darling, this way!" Ria wiggled about so that Lan Martak had no other choice. In a rush, he finished. As always, he felt drained from the intense erotic activity, but unlike the earlier times with Ria he now felt nothing more than physical tiredness. The spiritual thrill had gone. There hadn't been emotional involvement for over a week. And Ria seemed to be performing, to be demanding more of him not through love or even simple lust but because of some hidden need to stage a choreographed play.

Lan felt Ria's hot breath gusting across his chest. Her cheek pressed to his sweaty flesh in a way that now revolted him. Her fingers roved his body, teasing and toying with him in ways designed to arouse. Lan Martak experienced only disgust with what he had become—again.

Once before, when he'd come into a cask of jewels, wealth had altered his view of the world, changed his personality, made him into something he wasn't. He had almost lost his—and Inyx's—life because of the foolishness rising from inside due to the riches. This time he became no less the fool, but in a different way. He possessed no wealth but he controlled it. All he had to do was ask and he received. Hardly having two coins to clink together, Lan Martak still commanded a mansion, a beautiful, wanton, willing serving girl, the finest of clothing and food, anything he desired.

Again wealth had trapped him.

Lan's only consolation lay in the fact that this

time it was not mere wealth that drew him. As fine as the bed—and bedding—had been that first night, he would have moved on to seek out Inyx and to actively oppose Claybore if the magics around him hadn't gently coerced him to stay. Nothing blatant had shoved him down next to Ria; the pressures were soft, easy, barely noticeable.

Lan's magic sensing ability almost screamed at him now. He had noticed a honing of his skills in this regard and, while he could sense the spells, he lacked the acumen to do anything about them.

Puzzled, he glanced about the bedroom. Only Ria beside him, sleeping, caused the least disturbance. Lan disengaged himself from the woman's arms and sat up, drawn to the doorway by the intensity of the magic. In the arched doorway he felt the titanic flow around him. The diamonds embedded in the walls glowed with inner light. Lan pressed his hands to them. The diamonds were neither cold nor hard.

His hands fastened to the pulsating gems, Lan entered the river of magic and went with it. He initiated nothing; the magic pulled him along. He tried to move away, to fight, and found himself unable to change his course. Relaxing, he dived headfirst and went with the tides of magic around him. Carried up and away from his mansion, he floated toward Nashira's palace. The magics emanating from her audience chamber radiated like a yellow beacon in the night. He followed them down, down, down into the chamber itself.

"More wine," cried Nashira, presiding over the orgy. "Let us drink while our hero relieves himself!"

Lan turned to see the giant screen on the far wall. Ria's sleeping face almost filled it. Nashira and the others thought he had left the red-haired woman's side to answer a call to nature; they didn't know he—his spirit—viewed their activities.

"Come, come, Clete," chided Nashira from her throne, "not so clumsy with Aludra. Don't you remember how our hero did it? There, yes, shift your hips over. That's the position. Now pleasure her!"

Aludra groaned. Clete thrust. The watching crowd burst into a frenzy of erotic activity. It became apparent to Lan what happened. These nobles of Melitarsus were so jaded that they required voyeurism to consummate their own sexual needs. He had been nothing more than a trained dog performing for their pleasure.

Nashira clapped her hands. Her son Kyle led out a creature hardly larger than a dog but with a single blunted horn on its nose. The boy forced the animal to kneel while his mother hiked her skirts. She lowered herself onto the horn, a look of supreme excitement on her face.

"Now, Kyle, loose the beast now!"

The animal bucked and twisted under her. The Suzerain of Melitarsus kept her hips firmly pressed downward onto the horn. Lan felt his stomach beginning to churn in disgust. Whether it was at the woman's behavior or the expression of stark arousal on young Kyle's face, he didn't know. Nothing about Melitarsus was as it seemed. This decadent city and its ruler had used him—and he had allowed it.

The spells, at first, hadn't been strong enough to keep him. The lure of beautiful women and an easy life had almost been enough.

"What's keeping him?" demanded Nashira. "Ria must get him into action again. I need to watch them!"

Lan jerked his hands off the diamonds. He felt as if the skin ripped free, leaving raw wounds, but when he looked only normally callused flesh remained. The wounds were psychic. He turned back to the stirring Ria. Nashira had issued some un-spoken command to the serving girl, rousing her, demanding further sex play for the Suzerain's amusement.

"Lan, my love, come back to bed. Join me and I shall show you the wonders of the four thousand and fourth position." Her arms reached out for him, inviting milky-skinned arms meant to hold a man close. He fought the attraction as he knelt beside her.

"I want more than that, Ria. We have been too gentle. I demand more from you."

Her eyes shot open.

"What do you mean, my master?"

"You take me for granted. I must punish you for that."

"Master!"

He jerked her hand away from his groin and pulled her erect. With a smooth motion, he spun her around and bound her hands with the red silk sash from her dressing gown.

"Kneel!" he commanded.

"Yes, master. Wh-what are you going to do to me?"

"I haven't decided yet," he lied, gathering his clothing and weapons. "I don't think I want you to see, though, when I do decide." He blindfolded the redhead and pulled her along behind him.

"Where are we going, master? We shouldn't leave this room."

That told Lan much. This must be the only room Nashira had rigged with the magical seeing eyes. He'd have to provide Nashira and the others watching some alibi for his movement, or magical spells he couldn't counter would force him back.

"I want to see how you perform with animals. We're going to the stables."

"Animals, master?" Ria shivered. "But why do you keep me tied like this?"

"I enjoy it. Now be silent or I shall gag you, too." He pulled the bound, naked woman from the room and guided her through the silent corridors of the mansion. He hoped his hints as to what he intended would keep Nashira busy with her unicorn and the others similarly engaged long enough.

On the way to the stables, he stopped by Krek's quarters. The spider hung upside down in the middle of the room, eyes open, tears dripping from the corners.

"Don't say a word, Krek," warned Lan. "Just come with me."

The spider obeyed. He performed a quick twist in midair, landed on all eight legs, and trotted after Lan and Ria to the stables.

"Is someone with us, master?"

"Quiet, wench. I'm going to bind you to a post so you won't flinch."

"Flinch? You're not going to whip me, are you, master?" She either played the game well or actually wanted him to abuse her. She was going to be terribly disappointed, if the latter, or furious that she'd failed in her playacting, if the former. Lan bent her over a railing and tied her legs wide apart. With her hands still bound behind her back, she remained doubled up over the wooden rail.

"Where's the horse whip?" Lan asked. Krek's eyes widened, but the spider said nothing. Lan didn't seek out any whip. He got the tack needed for riding. He began saddling a strong mare.

"You're not going to whip me, are you master?" Ria's question came more as a demand.

"No, I decided against that," Lan said. "I'm going to allow the horse to have his will." He didn't even bother checking to see if any of the horses were stallions. It didn't matter. He'd already saddled and was ready to ride.

"No, please don't!" came the words, but the tone indicated excitement.

"You're too eager," snapped Lan. "I am going to let you think about what I'm going to do to you. For an hour I'm going to leave you blindfolded and tied like that. If you so much as move in that time, you'll live to regret it."

"Master!"

Lan Martak motioned for his spider companion to leave. Leading the horse outside, Lan closed the stable door behind them. He vaulted into the saddle and indicated that they should flee at top speed. Only when they were a full mile from the opulent mansion did Lan rein in and allow Krek to speak.

"You know everything, then, friend Lan Martak," said the spider.

"I've found out much in the past few hours. The grey-clad soldiers are flooding into Melitarsus."

"Not that, about Nashira, about her magics."

"I've discovered some of that, too, but I think I've only touched the surface. I've been unable to speak to her of Claybore and the greys. Some compulsion has prevented me—and it isn't Claybore's doing. Not this time. Nashira wants nothing to disturb her fantasy world." Lan paused, then shook his head sadly before continuing. "My reluctance to leave Melitarsus comes as much from Nashira's magic as it does from inner weakness."

"Yes, you must fight your longing for creature comfort. That is a true and deep flaw in your character."

"Thanks," Lan said dryly. "But I didn't see you making any attempt to leave. Did you like your web so much? The bugs they fed you?"

The entire body shivered and shook until Lan thought Krek might come apart.

"Oh, woe unto me, Lan Martak!" wailed the spider. "She put a geas on me so that I could not speak of it, not to anyone, even you. Even now, away from the nexus of her power, I find it difficult to tell of my bloody hours in the arena."

"What?" Lan was startled. Krek often seemed cowardly, but that was only his way. To be in an arena boggled the mind.

"The spell forced me to fight. I've killed hundreds in the past week, and all for her pleasure."

"Nashira's pleasures aren't those of other humans," Lan said grimly. He'd discovered that firsthand this evening. "Let's not talk about it. I only bought us an hour or so with Ria. When I don't show up to continue the performance, she'll know something's wrong. I think Nashira and her nobles are occupied enough to let us get out of the city. But we must hurry. Her powers seem limited to the confines of the city. Escape Melitarsus and we should be free of her spells."

"I quite agree, friend Lan Martak."

They hadn't travelled a quarter-mile when the grey-clad soldiers ambushed them.

The first warning Lan had was a man dropping from an overhanging branch and landing on the horse behind him. Strong hands grabbed his tunic and jerked to one side. Lan and the soldier fell heavily.

Lan recovered, rolled, kicked out, and entangled the man's feet. This gave Lan enough time to draw his sword.

"Rogue!" cried the soldier he faced. "You violate our curfew. For that you will die!"

Lan took that in, deciding the grey soldiers didn't recognize him. Claybore had to have put out a call—and a reward—for his capture of death. As long as the grey he faced didn't know his identity, he had a chance.

The chance faded instantly as a light shone into Lan's face. Another of the soldiers held a lantern high over his head to illuminate the battle scene.

"What! Why, you're—" The soldier got no further with the identification. A long sword drove directly through his throat. A bloody gurgling noise sounded a fraction of a second before blood geysered forth from severed arteries.

"Kill him. He's slain Willim! Kill the bastard!"

The other soldiers ringed Lan. He circled, thrusting tentatively to keep them at bay. They were well trained and made no mistakes. He faced a solid wall of deadly steel. He was in a difficult situation, but it could have been worse; none of the soldiers carried firearms from his home world. If they had, he'd be cooling meat in seconds.

"Willim stumbled onto my blade," he said, more to keep them off balance than to convince. "It was an honest mistake."

The one in front lunged, the tip of the blade snaking past Lan's guard to pink his wrist. Another thrust and hot pain blasted into his side. Still another slashed, opening a cut just above his riding boot. If they continued in this calculated fashion, he'd be cut to bloody ribbons in a few seconds.

"Hold, wait," came the command from the grey-clad holding the lantern. "This is the one Commander k'Adesina wishes. Look closely. Willim recognized him. That's why he killed him!"

"A prize catch. We'll live well off the reward for this one."

Lan parried and thrust. He missed. While off balance, two others added their cuts to his body.

"Krek!" Lan cried. "Help me!"

"Listen to him. You'd think he had an army with him."

"There's supposed to be another, a woman," said the commander. "Do you think . . ." His words died when Krek appeared. The spider hadn't been able to maintain the pace set by Lan's stolen horse. He'd finally caught up.

The momentary panic shown by the soldiers allowed Lan to put three of them out of action. The others spun to the attack.

And Krek simply stood.

"Krek, help me. I can't fight them all by myself. There's too many of them." Lan fended off a vicious attack, riposted, then used his knife to skewer an unwary grey-clad. Still, even reducing their ranks by four, they outnumbered and outpowered him.

"Oh, woe, I have killed so many. I have failed. I have taken lives for no reason."

"Krek, they'll kill me!" screamed Lan. "Are you going to help me or not?"

Seeing that the spider simply stood and didn't move to attack, the grey-clad soldiers concentrated on Lan. He succeeded in getting the tree trunk to his back, but this didn't slacken the attack from the five soldiers confronting him. His arms grew tired from parrying their strong attacks. His body grew increasingly bloody from the shallow cuts they inflicted. None was serious by itself, but the large number of scratches bled profusely. Without a miracle, he'd weaken and die.

"Krek, it wasn't your fault. She made you fight. She put you under a spell. It was Nashira's fault!"

He turned a lunge directly for his midsection, riposted, and buried his sword halfway into the soldier's belly. This proved Lan's undoing. His blade hit bone and twisted from his grip. He'd killed one attacker; he stood armed only with a knife against four others.

"Do you think so?" came Krek's whining voice.

"Yes, dammit, yes, it was Nashira's fault. She forced you!"

"Hmmm," mused the spider.

Lan Martak closed his eyes and waited for cold steel to rip through his torso, to spill real blood onto the dry earth. A scurrying noise sounded, confusing his mental image of the grey-clad soldiers' progress. When no killing blow landed, he opened his eyes. All four of the greys lay on the ground, arms severed, bodies cut in half, one decapitated. The commander's lantern stood to one side, casting a yellow glow on the grisly scene.

"That *did* feel different," commented Krek. "I killed for a reason, *my* reason."

"You killed to save me. There wasn't any pleasure in it."

"Oh, but there was. I enjoyed it. But I did it on my own, not because Nashira held me in her sway."

"Great. Let's get out of here. We've still got to get outside the walls before she learns we've gone. I don't know what spells she has at her command. Or what her son can do."

"Kyle?" asked Krek in his mild voice. "A most strange hatchling. Old beyond his years."

Lan grunted as he climbed once again into his saddle. If they had to fight another pitched battle, he didn't think he'd survive. As he rode, he tried to bind the worst of his cuts. None proved serious, but all were paining him greatly by the time they reached the great wall enclosing Melitarsus.

"This is a good spot," said Krek. "We can scale it here." A long strand of his sticky web-stuff shot upward and caught on an outjutting at the top of the wall. He began walking up the sheer rock front as easily as if he crossed a room.

"Krek, what about me?"

"Oh, I shall send down a strand for you once I reach the top."

"I need the horse. We'll never be able to get far enough away if I have to walk."

"You humans," sighed the spider. "If you had a proper number of legs, your travelling would be ever so much more pleasant and rapid."

"You go on up. Wait for me on the other side of the wall. I'll find a postern gate and get out that way." Lan waited until Krek reached the top of the wall, then spurred his horse on, going south toward a spot he remembered from his first day in Melitarsus. Once he sighted a flyer silently soaring through the night. The soft whistle of wind as it caressed the long, thin wings caused Lan to stop and wait. The white scarf worn by the pilot lashed back in the breeze, caught silver moonbeams. The flyer sailed on, oblivious to what happened a hundred feet below. Lan let out a sigh of relief and hurried on. He had to find the way out before the flyer or one of the guards spotted him or Krek. Less than ten minutes' riding brought him to a small, locked gate.

He dropped off and applied his knife point to the lock. The stubborn metal grated and ground and refused to open.

"What are you doing?" came the rough question. Guiltily, Lan spun to face one of the wall guards.

"Heard something on the other side. Wanted to see what happened there."

"This gate's always locked. Nothing but 'hoppers on the other side." The guard's eyes narrowed as he studied Lan. The adventurer's bloody clothing, the obvious signs of a recent fight, the knife working on the inner mechanism of the lock, all eventually penetrated the dull guard's mind.

"You're trying to escape!" he cried.

Lan Martak was in no condition to fight. He flicked his wrist and sent his knife cartwheeling toward the man. The knicked blade caught the guard in the upper arm. He howled in pain. Then came silence, after Lan's meaty fist knocked the man out. Using his knife again to cut up the guard's uniform, Lan took the strips and securely bound him. He was sick of killing, of bloodshed. Melitarsus thrived on it; its ruler required gore on a daily basis. He refused to further feed Nashira's sick needs. After all, this man only did his duty.

Lan dragged the bound, unconscious guard out of sight. As he did so, he felt a thick ring of keys. Taking them, he tried one after another until one unlocked the gate.

Krek waited on the other side, docilely munching on one of the large 'hoppers.

"Old spider, old friend, let's get away from this place before they think of new ways of holding us. The combination of sorcerer and flyer would be more than I could handle in my condition."

"I quite agree," said the spider. "And, friend Lan Martak, the veriest traces of Nashira's geas still remain on me. Watch me carefully in case it pulls me back to Melitarsus."

"The further we get from the city, the less hold the spell will have." Even as he spoke, Lan muttered counters he had learned on a world far away—his home.

Like chains breaking, the last vestiges of Nashira's binding spells fell away. Lan sucked in a deep, clean breath of air. It smelled of freedom. They hastened toward the distant crag of Mount Tartanius —and Claybore.

CHAPTER SIX

They rode hard all the first day, then had to stop to forage. Lan wished they'd had time to prepare more carefully for the road, but quickness in escaping Melitarsus had outweighed other concerns. He even chided himself for not stealing one of the Maxwell's demon-powered vehicles. While the demons were cantankerous, the speed they generated far exceeded that of a horse.

A vague fluttering of magic behind them provided the only indication that Nashira tried to stop them; by the time Lan sensed the spell, they had travelled well beyond its effective range. Still, Krek fed well on the grasshoppers and Lan had little trouble trapping an occasional rabbit. The 'hoppers had pretty well stripped the countryside bare of foliage to rob Lan of any greens in his diet, but this seemed a small price to pay to be free of Nashira.

"Friend Lan Martak," said Krek, slowly munching a 'hopper carcass, "I see a cloud of dust in the distance."

Lan spun and squinted. Riders. From Melitarsus.

"Damn, I didn't think they would follow. Nashira must value us more than I thought."

The spider shook like a leaf in a high wind at the thought of returning to the arena. He discarded his bug meal and rose up on all eight of his coppery-furred legs.

"They will not take me back. I can reach the Sulliman Range before they catch up, I can elude them forever. No human can catch me in mountains."

The mountains loomed purple and huge in the distance. Lan wondered how many more days travel lay before them. If they stayed on the road, their pursuers would overtake them before too long. He had no stomach for fighting off another armed band—if he were even able to do so. His cuts had begun healing, and he often helped the process along with a few healing chants he'd learned. In a way, this didn't work to his advantage. His wounds healed, but the use of even so minor a magic spell tired him greatly. He had no formal training in the arcane arts.

"If we head off parallel to the mountains, we might confuse them for a while," he told his large companion. "We can buy enough time to figure out some way around them."

"If we run away from the mountains, it only compounds our dilemma. Do we not need to make the utmost of haste to reach them? If so, then why dally?" The spider bobbed up and down, his eyes fixed on the distant dust cloud.

"We can't outrun them."

"I can."

"Then go on, dammit," snapped Lan, irritated. "Go on and leave me to fight them all by myself."

"Very well," said the spider complacently. Sarcasm was lost on Krek.

"Wait, wait," protested Lan. Without the spider's aid, he had no chance of ever again finding Inyx or combatting Claybore, much less tending to more immediate needs like fighting off their pursuers. "Maybe we can compromise on this."

"Why? You already told me to go on."

"Let's do it fast, then. I don't want to be caught in the open by those soldiers."

Lan saddled his horse and trotted alongside Krek, all the while turning over various schemes in his mind. A pitched battle was out of the question. He

wasn't up for it physically. Whether or not Nashira
sent along enough magics to subdue him was also
a problem to be contended with. She'd shown herself expert in coercive spells; if she turned Krek
against him, for instance, all was lost.

Yet Lan didn't think that to be any real worry.
From what he'd seen of Nashira, she might be
peeved for a time at his departure, then would go
on to other things. Melitarsus was a decadent city.
Decadent people had little time for long-standing
grudges. Living for the day was too important,
unless the momentary flash of hatred brought some
new fire to their lives.

Lan Martak shrugged it off. He couldn't plan
when he knew too little. The terrain changed grad-
ually from the meadows and plains to more rocky
expanses. Soon enough, huge boulders bulged from
the ground and the soil turned thin and barely able
to support life. With the decrease in vegetation
came a slackening of the grasshoppers. They remained where the foraging was the best; the rocky
foothills of the Sulliman Range wasn't to their
liking.

"Let's rest for a while," said Lan. "This old nag
is getting tired." And so was he, though he didn't
like to admit it to the seemingly tireless spider.
Krek couldn't keep up with a gallop, but his stam-
ina far outpaced the mare's over longer distances
at slower speeds. Lan dismounted and led the horse
to a small pond of water fed by an artesian spring.
After allowing the horse to drink for a minute, he
pulled the animal away and tethered her nearby.
Then he sated his own thirst.

"Come look, friend Lan Martak," called the spider. Krek had jumped from the floor of the gulch
in which they travelled to the top of a large rock
with one easy jump. His taloned feet clacked against
the rough brown rock, but other than this there

hadn't been any indication of strain on his part.

Lan wasn't so lucky. He struggled up the curve of the rock, fighting against treacherously loose gravel and leaving enough skin behind to start a new body. When he reached the summit the sight chilled him to the core of his being.

"Those aren't Nashira's men," he said in a low, choked voice.

"They do seem to be Claybore's grey-clad soldiers," agreed Krek.

Their pursuers weren't likely to drag them back to Melitarsus for further display. The greys would kill them on the spot.

"How do you think they found our trail?"

The spider twitched in wordless reply.

Lan thought hard. While he hadn't made it any secret that they travelled for Mount Tartanius, only Nashira had been told that outright. Others of her court might have overheard, or she might have mentioned it to them, but what did it matter how the grey-clad soldiers had found out? That they were only a day's ride behind was all that counted.

"This might be coincidence," said Lan, after considering various possibilities. "If Mount Tartanius is Claybore's base on this world, they might only be returning."

"Do you believe that?"

"Not for an instant," Lan admitted grimly. The sorcerer wasn't stupid, by any means. He'd realize that Lan and Inyx had become separated and, if they wanted to rejoin forces, would have to rally at some point. The cenotaph atop Mount Tartanius surfaced as the most likely spot, for a number of reasons. If they wanted off the world, they had to use that cenotaph. Lan hadn't found any other. Not knowing the world, the cenotaph provided the only unique spot that would attract attention. Hence,

Claybore had to have reasoned that Lan, Krek, and Inyx headed for the summit of the mountain.

"We can't let them report back, Krek. We've got to stop them."

As he stared at the clump of grey dots moving along the road, he wondered how they'd do that. All he had was a sword, a nicked knife, sore muscles, and an oversized spider prone to fits of depression.

Their future didn't look bright.

"We go away from the mountains," protested Krek. "How can we ever scale the loftiest of those peaks without first approaching them?"

"Krek," said Lan patiently, "we've got to get rid of the greys on our trail. If we don't, they'll soon enough overtake us."

"We can drive them off," said the spider.

"That's not good enough. If even one escapes, he'll report back to Claybore. That'll bring an entire regiment out. Claybore has more men than we can kill. We have to buy time."

"To scale Mount Tartanius?"

"Yes," Lan said, his patience beginning to wear thin. "So we'll stop the grey-clads following us now and hope that Claybore won't require them to report back regularly."

"I am not a simpleton," sniffed the spider. "You do not have to speak to me as if I were a child."

"Can you sling a web across this gulley?"

Krek eyed the distance critically, then bobbed his head in assent.

"Then do it!" Lan felt like screaming. The pressure of being pursued wore him down, and the giant arachnid's sense of values drove him to the brink of insanity.

"You need not be so gruff about it."

A hissing noise filled the air, and a long, sticky

strand of web-stuff dangled from one side of the ravine to the other. In the sunlight, gleaming rainbows danced off the strand. If Lan calculated properly, the sun would be setting when the greys rode down this ravine. They wouldn't see the strand until it hit them at shoulder level.

He hoped.

Lan fixed a small dinner, ate in silence, worried. Krek hovered nearby, his movements jerky and nervous. Neither of them waited particularly well. Lan was on the point of commenting about that when the first distant sounds of hooves on rock reached him.

"They're coming."

"Six of them," said the spider, his claws shoved down hard onto the rock. He sensed the vibrations made by the horses and interpreted it with great accuracy. "They arrive in a few minutes. Are you ready, friend Lan Martak? I have no stomach for more wanton killing."

"Your strand's still up?"

"Of course," the spider said disdainfully. "My hunting webs always stay up until my prey is trapped. You are a fine one to criticize my expertise. Who was it who—"

"Quiet!"

The horses galloped forward. Lan stood, slipping both sword and knife from their sheaths. He stood in the center of a sandy pit, waiting, ready. His hands shook slightly when he saw the dark figures outlined against the setting sun. Everything rested on the attacking soldiers' not seeing Krek's web.

The commander of the patrol waved a free hand. They galloped forth, screaming, cheering, proclaiming their victory. Lan listened to their cries and shuddered. Claybore had promised vast rewards for his capture. That made him feel warm inside, knowing that he posed such a threat to the powerful mage. It also chilled him. These soldiers wouldn't retreat now that they'd found him.

"Surrender, dog!" cried the nearest.

Lan stood and said nothing.

The front three came thundering between the rocks. For a split second, nothing happened. Then the three dangled in midair, their horses continuing on without them. The men fought desperately to escape the sticky strand of hunting web. The more they struggled, the more entangled they became.

Those three wouldn't contribute to the fight; the remaining three avoided the web, ducking beneath and racing past.

"Here goes nothing," said Lan, bracing himself. He slashed out, not even attempting for chivalry. His life depended on this contest. His sword caught the lead rider's horse squarely in the chest. The horse let out a wet cough, then somersaulted, taking the soldier with it. Rider and horse were out of action, but Lan lost his sword, which remained buried to the hilt in the animal's chest. He faced two mounted and armed greys with only a knife.

"Surrender, fool, or we'll spit you like a pig," barked the one nearest.

"Is talk all you have to offer?" said Lan. He took a desperate chance. His knife spun through the air. For a heart-stopping instant, Lan thought the knife had missed its tiny target. The man sat upright in his saddle, then slumped. The blade had flown true and buried point first in his right eye. An impossible throw, but luck finally turned in Lan's favor.

"That leaves us," he said to the remaining grey. He'd never figured out the ranking system the soldiers used. This one had four red stripes and a star on the left sleeve—and a glinting saber in the right hand. The setting sun caught the cutting edge of the sword and turned it blood-red, an omen Lan Martak didn't care for.

The soldier attacked without voicing any warning. There was hardly any need. They both knew that one of them would die.

Lan ducked at the last moment, the saber cutting through the air above his head. He launched himself upward, groping for the grey. Fingers slipped off cloth, and he landed on the horse's haunches. Only an agile twist carried him away before the animal's hind legs kicked out.

The soldier spun and came at him again.

"Krek, do something!" he shouted to his companion. The spider cowered at the perimeter of the sandy pit, hunkered down into a brown lump indistinguishable from any of the other rocks in the twilight.

"I cannot, friend Lan Martak. I quiver at the memory of the torment I have caused."

"Nashira forced you, Krek. It wasn't your fault," argued Lan. The next attack caught him flatfooted. Heavy steel blade slapped alongside his head. Dazed, he dropped to his knees, neck exposed. As the grey came back for the killing blow, the spider rose up to full height. The horse shied, bucked, tossed its rider. Blowing foam, the animal charged back down the ravine in the direction it had come.

"I can do no more," came the baleful words.

Lan's fingers tightened on a fallen sword. He didn't know who it had belonged to, nor did it matter. It hefted poorly, out of balance, and it didn't matter. He had a fighting chance again. Still shaky, he got to his feet and faced the remaining soldier.

Lan Martak had no chance to come en garde. He blocked a clumsy saber slash, turned, and found himself wrestling on the ground.

"I will never surrender!" cried the soldier in a

high voice. Lan saw that the officer he fought was a woman. For an instant, he slackened his attack. She twisted like a tiger, drove her knee upward into his belly, then punched for his throat.

He caught a slender wrist and forced it behind her back. Holding her in an armlock, he finally caught his breath.

"Stop it or I'll break your arm off and beat you to death with it," he warned.

Her struggles lessened, but the tenseness remained.

"Kill me, if you will, but there are others. Many others. You will die, lover of animals."

Lan frowned. Her intensity spoke of personal hatred. He'd seen soldiers doing their duty and nothing more, soldiers devoted to their leaders, soldiers passionately involved in their assignments, but none had ever carried the personal hatred this woman did.

"Do I know you?" he asked.

"Pig!"

"It seems she is lacking in knowledge of anatomy," commented Krek. "She has mistaken you for one of your porcine cousins." The spider lurched over and stood before the woman. "You see, dear lady, this fellow is possessed of only two legs, not unlike yourself. He—"

"Krek," snapped Lan, impatient. "She knows biology. That was intended as an insult. I'm trying to find out why."

"Oh." The spider sank to the ground and watched the imponderable humans go about their odd mating rituals.

"I could die happily knowing I'd sent you to the Lower Places, Lan Martak."

"You know my name. That's not surprising since Claybore has put out a sizable reward for me. I overheard you mention it just before your squad attacked."

"I'd skewer you for free!"

"So," Lan went on, never lessening his hold on the woman's arm, "you know me personally. The reward doesn't matter. Yet I've never seen you before in my life. Why do you hate me so?"

"You killed Lyk Surepta."

Lan Martak relaxed his grip in shock at the words. The soldier spun, kicked him, and went for his throat. It took another full minute of struggling to again bring her under control.

"What was Surepta to you?" Lan's voice hardened at the memory of the grief that man had caused him. Run him out of his home, killed both lover and half-sister, tried to rape Inyx—the indictment against Surepta was impressive. Lan felt no regret at having killed the man.

"My husband!" The woman tried to spit in Lan's face. He held her shoulders pinned to the ground with his knees. With one hand he turned her jaw enough so that she could neither bite nor spit. "I'll avenge his foul murder!"

"I had no idea Surepta was married. From his raping, he didn't act like it."

"Lies!"

"Did he meet you in Waldron's service?"

"Yes."

Lan mentally filled in the story. He'd certainly never get it from this unwilling woman. Surepta had been given a generalship in Waldron's army of conquest—in reality, Claybore's army—and had met this spitfire. They'd married, and Lan had killed Surepta for all his crimes. Waldron or someone close to him had told her who was responsible. She now took it on herself to personally vindicate her husband's death.

Lan knew it would do no good trying to dissuade

her. Her mind had become fixed on revenge. It'd do even less good to tell her he'd gotten no particular thrill out of Surepta's death. He'd killed and hadn't enjoyed the vengeance.

"What's your name?"

"Kiska k'Adesina. I want you to know the name of your killer, pig!"

"She still has you confused with the cloven-hoofed—"

"Shut up, Krek." Lan peered down at the woman. Somehow, he couldn't believe Surepta had married her. It mattered little. Kiska k'Adesina was driven by revenge, whatever the cause. She had mouse-brown hair, now dirtied and matted, brown eyes that might be lovely if the hatred ever died in them, a thin-lipped mouth, delicate bones and a slightly curving nose, a long, slender neck and a svelte build that might be seductive if she wore other than the grey uniform. He remembered the half-seen grey commander in Melitarsus, outside the inn. He'd wondered briefly then; now he knew. He held Claybore's commander in his arms. "The spider is hardly an expert. His wife's trying to eat him," Lan said, trying to soften the mood. His brief overture to her didn't work.

"A woman must defend her husband. You're a dead man, Lan Martak."

He heaved a sigh. What to do with Kiska k'Adesina proved a problem. He could hardly kill her in cold blood. He hadn't the stomach for that. Letting her loose only meant more trouble. Either she'd dog his trail trying to slay him or she'd report back to Claybore. The sorcerer wouldn't make any mistakes this time. Lan was as good as dead if Claybore located him.

"I can cocoon her, like the others, friend Lan Martak," piped up Krek, as if reading the man's mind. "She will free herself eventually."

"Before she died of hunger or thirst?"

The spider quivered, giving his equivalent of a shrug. Lan wasn't enthused with this solution, but it provided the most effective means of keeping k'Adesina out of his hair—and without wantonly murdering her. No matter what she thought, he wasn't a killer. Fight in self-defense, yes, but not a cold-blooded murderer.

In that respect, he wasn't like her dead husband, Lyk Surepta.

"Ready, Lan?" he asked. When he saw the spider's answering head-bob, he released the woman. She rolled, got to her feet, and tried to flee. A long, sticky strand of web-stuff tangled her legs. In less than five minutes she hung suspended between two rocks, her arms and legs securely glued under copious layers of silk.

"Leaving her thusly will prevent wild animals from sampling her flesh," said Krek. "It works quite well in the Egrii Mountains. We often have food for our hatchlings stored away for months."

"You'll die, Lan Martak," she cried. "I'll see your filthy heart cut out for all you've done."

"Let's ride, Krek," he said. Nothing he said to the woman would have any effect. Perhaps dangling in her silken prison for a few days—a week?—might lessen her hatred. But he doubted it.

Lan Martak rode off, the feeling of Kiska k'Adesina's eyes boring into his back. How long would it be before she managed to exchange a simple look of hatred for a steel dagger? Lan didn't want to think about it. Too much lay ahead.

Mount Tartanius.

And Claybore.

CHAPTER SEVEN

"Will she die, do you think?" asked Lan of his companion. He turned in the saddle to see the spider wiggling his head from side to side. That didn't tell the human anything. The spider's gait had changed as the terrain became progressively rockier. This might signify added effort in walking rather than an affirmative answer to the question.

"Well?" he pressed.

"You mean the woman soldier?"

"Of course, I do. Who else?"

"It is often difficult following your meaning. You humans have thought processes that are decidedly inferior to arachnids'."

"Don't give me your half-baked philosophy. Give me your opinion."

"She will probably escape. The cords binding her were not unduly tight, nor altogether well wrapped. In my opinion, you should have eaten her."

Lan shuddered, thinking of spiderish mores. Such cannibalism as Krek so casually mentioned was a part of everyday life in the insect kingdom. Lan hadn't even been able to bring himself to leave the woman with her throat slit, though she'd've done such a thing to him gladly.

"The other three will be longer in getting free. I spun extra adhesive onto their bonds. They maligned me."

"Oh," said Lan, interested and happy to get his mind off his problems and onto something else. "What did they say?"

"I prefer not to repeat such vile calumnies."

"You didn't do anything like fasten the cords around their necks, did you?"

"That spindly stick holding up their heads? No, friend Inyx dissuaded me from doing that some time ago."

"Inyx," said Lan aloud, then regretted it.

"You miss her, friend Lan Martak?"

"Yes. With her along I doubt we'd have gotten into half the predicaments we had."

"Her counsel is wiser," agreed the spider. Lan felt no joy in hearing the arachnid confirm it, though.

"Do you still 'see' the cenotaph atop Mount Tartanius?"

Krek stopped, rotated his head until the human thought it might screw off, then bobbed up and down.

"It is there. A very strong one. That is why I believe it might be the Kinetic Sphere rather than a simple cenotaph joining worlds. From such a vantage point, Claybore could survey the entire planet."

"I don't think he's up there. The Kinetic Sphere might be, but not Claybore."

"Why do you say that?"

"He'd use the Sphere to come after us. We're the immediate danger facing him. I think, when I knocked it out of his hand between worlds, he was thrown elsewhere on this world. Something about the summit pulled the Kinetic Sphere, but the rest of us were strewn about."

"This is the tallest peak on the planet."

"We might be in a race to recover the Kinetic Sphere." Lan felt grim satisfaction in that thought. If he recovered the Sphere, that took away much of Claybore's power. The decapitated sorcerer still retained a potent store of magics, but the ability to shift worlds at random, without the use of a naturally occurring cenotaph, might stop his immediate plans for conquest. If the loss of the Kinetic Sphere didn't stop him, it slowed him drastically.

"If we are in a race, the track becomes more and more crowded. Look ahead."

Lan glanced up and saw a small encampment. Rude tents were pitched in a haphazard fashion, some of them even opening into the cruel wind blowing off the mountains. No drainage had been provided; a rain would wash the encampment down the slopes and into oblivion. Even elementary sanitation had been ignored.

"They're not much in the ways of roughing it. Think it might be some of Nashira's friends from Melitarsus?"

"They are too plainly dressed for that," said the spider. His eyes proved more acute than Lan's in the gathering gloom of evening.

"It's not going to do us any good trying to skirt them. They've spotted us. Look."

High atop a rock overlooking the camp stood a man dressed in a simple brown robe, the cowl tossed up to conceal his face. He flapped his arms like some giant, coarse bird unable to fly. Lan guessed he signalled them to approach.

They entered the camp amid the deathly silence of the gathered people. The only sound to be heard was wind howling through crags too distant to see in the darkness. A man tried to light a fire using steel and flint. He held both wrong; the sparks skittered into the night rather than onto the firewood. Lan felt the eyes peering at him, evaluating him. Whoever these people were, they weren't Claybore's troops. None of the grey-clad soldiers set camp in such slovenly fashion.

"Greetings," called out Lan. "We're travellers. Heading into the Sulliman Range."

"For what purpose?"

Lan tried to figure out which of the grim, brown-black figures had spoken. They remained anonymous under their hoods.

"We climb Mount Tartanius."

A sigh of relief passed through the throng. One by one, they slipped away until only one man remained. He tossed back his cowl and stared up at Lan. A tingle of dread passed through the mounted man. The eyes burned with an eerie inner light that made him uneasy.

A sputtering noise, followed by a loud hiss, frightened Lan's horse. By the time he'd controlled his mount, the firemaker had done his job, more by accident than design. A small campfire blazed, pushing back the velvet shadows. The new light did nothing to erase Lan's uneasiness about the man confronting him.

"I am Ehznoll," came the simple words.

"Am I supposed to know you?"

"I am a pilgrim."

"We are, too, in a way," explained Lan.

"We?"

Lan glanced around. Krek had sunk into the shadows of a nearby rock and merged with them.

"My friend is a bit shy. You don't hold anything against spiders, do you. Large ones?"

Ehznoll shook his head. Lan got the impression that nothing frightened this man. Not that courage had anything to do with it; fanatical intensity surrounded his every movement.

"Come on into the light, Krek. You don't have to get too close to the fire." To Ehznoll, he quietly explained, "My friend hates fire and water both."

"Welcome, pilgrims," intoned Ehznoll when Krek joined Lan. "You are entitled to a meal with us. If you desire, you may accompany us for we, too, are journeying to the summit of Mount Tartanius."

"For what reason?"

"For the holiest of reasons!" shrieked Ehznoll. He thrust his fist skyward. His followers stopped their activities and dropped to one knee, heads bent, wrists crossed and pressed to their breasts.

"I see," muttered Lan. "Our purposes are likewise noble."

"We go to look down upon the world that has created us. We worship the planet itself. The sky enfolds us, we hunger for dirt beneath our feet. Rejoice, pilgrims, we seek the dagger of the earth ripping asunder the enemy sky!"

A cheer went up from the twenty or so pilgrims. The few whose faces Lan could see had a transcendent expression. Whatever the tenets of this religion, they were totally devout. He didn't doubt for an instant they'd kill if either he or Krek voiced the slightest skepticism.

"You've come far?" asked Lan, hoping to keep Ehznoll talking. That seemed the least risky of his choices. As the man began a long tirade against the sky and for the planet, Lan dismounted and sat beside the fire. A tiny rabbit roasted. He hoped it wasn't intended to feed all those in camp.

"Across the face of this wonderous orb, spinning through hideous void, I've trekked with dirt under my feet, revelling in the sensations of our worshipful host." Ehznoll sat, pulled off his sandals, and displayed his feet for Lan's approval. It was all he could do to keep from gagging. Ehznoll's feet were festered with open, running sores. The dirt fell off in small cakes, and the man's jagged toenails rippled black in the faint campfire light. Lan turned away so that the smell wouldn't completely sicken him.

"These are my banners of piety. My feet have caressed the holy host and made it part of me." Ehznoll began putting on the sandals again. Lan finally chanced a quick breath. Only the cold, crisp mountain air reached his lungs.

"You venerate all dirt, then?" he asked.

"All," solemnly affirmed Ehznoll.

"Mount Tartanius is certainly a tribute to, uh, dirt," Lan said lamely. He found himself more and more at a loss to carry on the conversation. He knew if he said the wrong thing, Ehznoll would turn on him. The gleam of fanaticism in the man's eyes ensured that.

"You journey to the very summit, also?"

"We do."

"You are privileged."

"I know."

Ehznoll said nothing more. He went to the nearest tent, pulled back the tattered flap, and crawled inside. Lan shook his head in wonder. The brief glimpse he'd gotten showed no blanket or padding. Ehznoll slept next to the cold earth.

"The tent's to keep off the sky," supplied the man roasting the rabbit. "We have to stay close to the earth, especially during the hours of darkness. 'Tis easy to become subverted from the True Faith in the black pit of night."

"I can imagine," Lan said uneasily.

"Food?"

"If it's of the earth," Lan said.

The man shrugged, passed over a charred haunch of rabbit. Lan took it and ate slowly, the grease remaining running down his chin. He wiped it off, rather than wait until after he'd finished. The mere thought of dirt caking to his chin offended him mightily now. He'd have enough filth to contend with the next days as they climbed higher and higher up the slopes of Mount Tartanius.

His eyes turned to the towering mound of rock. It reached to the very vault of the diamond-studded night sky. Up there rested a cenotaph, either a properly consecrated grave without a corpse inside or the Kinetic Sphere, able to shift at random from world to world. Either way, a path to Inyx existed—and a way of stopping Claybore beckoned to him.

Lan finished gnawing on a slender bone, tossed it aside, then curled up next to Krek's hind legs. The spider gusted a sigh, twitched, then went back to sleep. Lan found the furry berth more reassuring than the spare tents pitched randomly across the slope of the foothills. In seconds, he slept.

"This seems like a poor idea, friend Lan Martak," complained Krek. "I do not know if I can tolerate another moment with these bigots."

"Just because they called you an unbeliever is no reason to get so belligerent."

"I *enjoy* swinging through space on the end of a properly spun strand. Nothing appeals to me more than to be up on a web, away from the foot-wearying dirt, relishing the freedom of emptiness all about me. How *dare* they claim I am the child of the demons?"

"Nothing personal, Krek," said Lan, trying to keep from laughing. Try as he might, he failed to hold back a broad smile. "They love their dirt."

"They are filthy."

Lan's nose twitched as the spider said that. Ehznoll had moved upwind. His body odor only accentuated the spider's opinion. Bathing violated the tenets of Ehznoll's religion. The removal of any sort of dirt from the body lessened one's touch with the godhead. Lan wondered if the spider and these zealots were of a common heritage; without a sense of smell, cleanliness took on a different connotation. Still, Krek valued a clean set of legs, a highly polished abdomen, neatly trimmed mandibles, the entire array of arachnid hygiene.

"Noonday prayers, noonday prayers!" bellowed Ehznoll from ahead.

"We must have located still another hog wallow. Perhaps it was Ehznoll that Kiska female mistook you for. There are definite porcine comparisons to draw between an unclean human and a pig in—"

"Quiet, Krek. Don't let them hear you. They're touchy enough."

"Let us push on. Why do we need to remain with such disreputable wights?"

"It's good camouflage for us. If the grey-clad soldiers come by, they'll only give this crew a passing glance. We become part of the pilgrimage, we get ignored. And since Ehznoll is heading in the same direction, to the same destination, it's ridiculous not to join forces. These are dangerous mountains. A group stands a better chance of survival than a mere pair." The spider began to bristle. Lan hurriedly added, "Even when half of the pair is a renowned Webmaster from the Egrii Mountains."

Krek calmed a little, but remained aloof while Ehznoll's band dropped to the floor of a small ravine and rolled about, rubbing the sand over their bodies. Lan hoped it might cleanse them; if anything, they emerged even more filthy.

Lan sat and rested. Much of the day he'd had to walk beside his mare instead of riding her. The path upward became more and more hazardous. Many times he'd almost twisted an ankle on loose stone. The horse walked more sure-footedly than he did but still had difficulty picking a solid path.

He closed his eyes and let his mind range wide. He drifted, almost falling asleep. In that half-and-half state, he saw a dim figure, a ghostly figure. He reached out. Inyx came forward, fear obvious in her expression. As his hand touched hers, she exploded in an actinic glare that blinded him. Left in her place, just above eye level, floated a skull.

Claybore's fleshless skull, eye sockets blackened and teeth chipped. The fleshless head turned and sought out Lan. Twin beams of ruby death flicked forth, tentative, unsure, seeking. Lan danced away in that nothingness. Neither he nor the sorcerer was supreme here.

The eye sockets blazed more vividly. Lan averted his gaze to keep from staring directly into the hollows. Instinctively he knew to do so meant death—worse. To be trapped and subjugated to Claybore's will ranked far worse than death.

"Lan," came the faint voice. "Where are you, Lan? I need you. Please come. Please!" The voice faded away. Inyx spoke to him, and he failed her.

"Inyx!" he cried aloud. "Where are you?"

"What?" came Krek's voice. "What is wrong?"

"I . . . nothing." He leaned back against the rock, feeling its cold massiveness sucking his body's warmth now. Sweat ran down his face. He had seen Claybore in that nothing world. Inside his head, a pressure had built until it felt as if he must burst like the overheated steam boiler on one of the demon-powered cars. Power was—almost—his. He had felt the magics flowing around them, had touched some of them.

And Inyx. Inyx remained lost between worlds. She hadn't escaped into this world when he'd batted the Kinetic Sphere from Claybore's grip. Only the sorcerer, he, and Krek had left the white limbo.

"Krek, we've got to get the Kinetic Sphere. Inyx is still trapped between worlds."

"How do you know?"

"My . . . my magic sensing." He almost stuttered, so great were the emotions wracking him. Lan knew things that he couldn't explain. The excursion through the ghostly whiteness had given birth to twitching, crawling things inside his head. "Inyx can't survive much longer."

"But Claybore has the Sphere."

"No," said Lan slowly. "I don't think he does. We truly are in a race to reach the summit. The Kinetic Sphere is up there." He pointed upward to the top of Mount Tartanius. "It landed there when it left the whiteness."

"How does Claybore travel? He lacks a body."

"But he's a powerful mage. Remember how he used Waldron? He must be using others. Or maybe . . ."

"Yes?"

"Maybe his powers are materially weakened by the shift between worlds. Maybe he needs the Kinetic Sphere for more than interworld travel. If he sucks power from it, being distant from the globe might sap his strength."

"Possible," conceded Krek, "though it is more likely he sits aloft and waits, like a proper spider in the center of a web."

"How apt your comparisons are today, friend spider," said Lan. "I think he races us for the summit. Whoever reaches the top of Mount Tartanius first wins the prize of the Kinetic Sphere."

"I prefer the thought of succulent grasshoppers."

"We could rescue Inyx."

"Hmmm," mused the spider. "I rather did like her. We share certain traits."

"Only a few, I trust," said Lan, remembering Krek's bride and her appetites.

"The best ones," Krek assured him.

Lan Martak looked from the dirt-rolling Ehznoll and his disciples up the craggy slopes of the Sulliman Range to the immense Mount Tartanius. Atop that peak lay more than his destiny. The destiny of worlds hung in the balance.

He'd reach the Kinetic Sphere first. He had to.

CHAPTER EIGHT

"It's closing in on me, Krek," Lan Martak cried in panic. He'd been dozing while riding and had another dream. Walls circled around, then began to crush him into pulp. Intense claustrophobia seized him; the times in his life when he'd been the most powerless were those times he'd been closed in. Trapped in the cellar while he listened to his half-sister being raped and murdered; accidentally locked in a trunk when a small child; stranded for fourteen days in a mine shaft he explored in the el-Liot Mountains; those were the horrific times of his life. Lan belonged in the open spaces, not simply because he loved it—he needed it. Being locked in not-so-slowly drove him insane.

"What? What closes in? The world is wide and beautiful, even if it is filled with debris like Ehznoll and his band."

Lan shivered. The dream had seemed closer to reality than the world did now. He glanced upward, toward the crest of Mount Tartanius. His magic sense tightened until he felt a knot in the pit of his stomach. As the days progressed, so did his feeling that some power grew within him. His magic sensing ability had become as sharp as a razor, as taut as a pulled wire. He felt ready to lash out, to explode under the tension.

"Up there. I feel it. I feel the power radiating from the top of the mountain."

"It *is* strong," said the spider. "I do believe it is the Kinetic Sphere. No mere cenotaph 'looks' quite

96

like it. It is little wonder even you can sense it. What is peculiar is an inability to do so."

"They don't sense it at all," said Lan. Ehznoll and his band frolicked in the dirt, flinging bits of dried mud at one another. They were anything but dour this day. Ehznoll had said something about its being a holiday for them, a day to rejoice and revel in their nearness to the earth. To Lan, they didn't seem to be doing any more than they had done on prior days.

"Little wonder," sniffed Krek. "It would take a major hosing down to even reach their skin. Their four physical senses are totally numbed by the layers of filth they wear like a cloak."

"Five senses."

"There you go again, prattling on about this elusive sense of smell. If it is anything like you describe it—and I believe it all a product of your twisted human mind—it gives you no advantage dealing with them."

"They can't sneak up on me."

"Nor can they on me." Krek flexed his long legs, tightening his grip on the rock until the tips of his talons penetrated the stone. He detected the most sensitive of vibrations in this fashion.

"Lan Martak!" called Ehznoll. "We stop for the remainder of the day. Join us in our frolics."

Lan dismounted and went to the pilgrim. He tried holding his breath against the oders emanating from the unkept man's robe. He fought a losing battle.

"I . . . I feel called. Krek and I should scout ahead."

"The good earth will not deceive us," spoke up a woman nearby. "Trust in the planet. The dirt will never leave us. We are the children of the earth."

"Never left the womb, either," muttered Krek from behind. Lan motioned for the spider to be silent.

"Just the same, we'll check out the route."

"Stay, stay and rejoice with us," the woman said, coming closer. Grimy fingers reached out to stroke Lan's cheek. He flinched. She didn't notice. Moving closer, she whispered in a husky voice, "We rejoice in many ways."

"Uh, isn't that against your tenets?"

"What? Making love?" she asked, surprised. As her eyebrows shot up, a tiny particle of dirt dislodged. Lan saw she had blonde hair rather than the dull brown caused by the dust and dirt. "Hardly. If anything, it is part of our most basic sacrament. If we aren't fruitful, how can we possibly ensure that the praise of our earth is carried on to future generations?"

"Don't most religions call for celibacy?" asked Lan. He backed up slightly and ran into Krek. The giant spider didn't move. He peered over the man's shoulder with intense interest.

"Is this part of the human mating ritual, also? You have such varied techniques, friend Lan Martak, that I am amazed. We mountain arachnids engage in much simpler courtship rites."

"And then your damn bride devours you!" blurted Lan.

Krek only shrugged, shivering all over.

"Take part in the rejoicing, stranger," the woman urged again. "I am one of the holiest."

"The dirtiest, you mean?"

"It's the same thing," cut in Ehznoll. "She is giving you singular honor. Melira is a standout, even in this devout band."

The woman had allowed her cowl to fall back. Hair hung in greasy strings on either side of her smudged face. Lips chapped, front tooth broken, dirt everywhere, she only repelled Lan instead of attracting him. When she shifted the coarse brown robe back and off her shoulders, holding the filthy garment in the crooks of her elbows and revealing her upper chest, he almost turned and ran. Only Krek's bulk prevented him from getting on his mare and riding until either he or the horse collapsed from exhaustion.

Her breasts swayed like pendulums, each with a slightly different frequency of oscillation. Dirt encrusted the upper slopes, and pink nipples poked through the grime. Lan's mind instantly flashed to what the rest of Melira's body would be like.

"I've taken a vow of celibacy," he said quickly.

"Indeed, friend Lan Martak, when was this?"

"Shut up, Krek. I, uh, took the vow because of the friend we're trying to find and rescue. Yes, that's it. I promised Inyx not to be with another woman."

"Is she so perverted?" asked Melira in what she considered a seductive voice. "Our cult allows free choice during each rejoicing. There are no permanent bonds. You are too attractive to merely sit on the sidelines and not take part."

"My vow is sacred. To me, to Inyx, to the earth."

Both Melira and Ehznoll sighed.

"So be it. A vow to the earth takes precedence."

It was Lan's turn to sigh—with relief. The pair turned and rejoined the tiny band of pilgrims, already stripping and kneeling to throw dirt on one another before they started serious praying.

"Let's get out of here. I don't want to even be around when they start—" The man stopped and stared at his friend. Krek stood rigidly, claws buried in the hard flint rocks. His eyes had glazed over, and rigor mortis might have set in for all the animation he showed. "What's the matter?"

"Big," came Krek's tiny voice. "Never seen—felt—anything like it. Huge!"

The way the spider inflected the words caused Lan to whip out his sword and peer about. He personally sensed no magics; that left Krek's vibration detection. Whatever so paralyzed the spider had to be dangerous.

"Is it the grey-clad soldiers? Has Kiska gotten loose and brought a company down on us?"

"No. Only one. But enormous!"

"Krek, tell me what it is. I . . . by the demons of the Lower Places!" Lan gasped and took an involuntary step backward. He craned his neck up—up—up—and saw only pincers emerging over a rock. Each pincer spanned almost four feet. His mare reared and kicked out futilely. Lan made no effort to calm her. In this battle the slightest misattention meant death.

More of the monster emerged. Lan irrationally thought back to the bog world where he'd saved Krek from wolves. He'd thought the eight-foot-tall spider to be a monster. The limpid dun-colored eyes, sometimes soft and forlorn, softened the image. Krek's personality also took away from the idea of the spider being a monster.

The *monster* crawling over the rock to tower over them took away his breath. The scorpion-creature topped Krek's eight feet by a sizable margin. Perhaps by as much as Lan's height. The hard-shelled torso looked strong enough to fend off anything short of a battering ram. A tiny head perched on the abdomen, eyes of only hatred peering forth.

"The stinger, watch out for the stinger," cried Krek.

The long tail arced over the scorpion's body, down past the head, and caught the mare squarely on the back. A loud snapping noise, the horse's hysterical neighs, then the sound of blood spilling forth. Death had come quickly for the animal.

"How do we fight it?" gasped Lan. He looked at

his fine steel sword. It might as well have been a toothpick against this beast.

Krek hopped away, bobbing and spinning a web. The spider fought his own battle. Seeing that Krek worked at a hunting web, Lan ducked and waved his sword high over his head in an attempt to distract the scorpion. If he won enough time for the spider to finish his sticky strands, they had a chance. Krek had once told him he'd caught and held a bear in those strands.

"Hey, hey, hey!" he called, jumping about as if he'd become quite insane. "This way." The scorpion's head followed his movement, but the body didn't stir. It needed a steady base for the proper use of the deadly stinger. Lan saw it coming. Reflexes saved his life. He parried with his sword at the last possible instant. Sparks leaped from his blade as the tail slid away harmlessly. But the impact had been so severe Lan's entire arm went numb with shock.

He backpedalled quickly to stay out of the range of a second stinger attack.

"What's wrong with you?" Lan demanded of Ehznoll. "Fight this damn thing. It'll kill us all!"

"It is a creature of the earth. We will pray for it."

"It'll kill you!"

"Our prayers to the godhead of earth will be answered. The planet will not allow us to die, not on this day of rejoicing, not under the awfulness of the empty sky. We are devout pilgrims; we will not be sacrificed in this manner."

Ehznoll and the others commenced praying. Lan stood in stunned silence and, one by one, they dropped to one knee, crossed wrists over their breasts, and began singing. The whine of a scorpion's tail slashing through the air made him leap without even looking. He hit the ground hard, rolled into flint, felt tiny cuts opening all over his still-paralyzed arm. In a way, the injuries aided him. Feeling—pain—came back to him more rapidly.

"Krek, hurry it up. This thing's starting to look hungry."

He stared up at the monster, the stinger poised directly over its head. A single drop of green fluid beaded there. Lan didn't have to be told this poison could immobilize any living creature. Scorpions of much smaller size paralyzed with the poison, then stored their meal away for future use.

As the stinger lashed downward again, a single wrist-thick strand of web-stuff rose to meet it. The sticky material clung but didn't hold back the tail. Krek continued to bind the scorpion, one strand at a time, until a dozen thick cords partially contained it, holding it down on the rock. The enraged scorpion let out a bellow more appropriate to a mountain lion and shook itself all over.

Webs popped as if the spider had used only common twine. Still, Krek didn't give up. More of his hunting web arched up to entangle the monster. It became a battle of technique. The scorpion was powerful enough to break all the bands—in time. Krek fought to put more on than the creature could burst at any given instant.

Lan watched in helpless fury. His friend fought the battle; he was little better than Ehznoll and his pilgrims. Still, even with feeling returned in his sword arm, what could he do? The most vital portions of the scorpion's anatomy lay a full yard above his furthest reach. Even if he'd dared, he didn't think a single sword capable of penetrating that exoskeleton.

"How long will he stay bound?" he called out to the spider.

"He breaks loose even as I spin the webs. Fleeing is out of the question. He moves too quickly to outrun."

"Keep him pinned down, Krek. I've got an idea."

The spider didn't answer; his full attention lay in combatting the scorpion. Lan Martak raced for the edge of the ravine, clambered up the side, then began the arduous climb up the rock face of the cliff overlooking the area. Each finger grip seemed incapable of holding his weight. Rock broke loose and tumbled downward. His knees skinned and hands bloody, Lan fought to climb the sheer rock face. Once he turned and glanced at the scene below. He was easily thirty feet up now; the scorpion dwarfed all below. Krek appeared a toy in comparison and the band of praying pilgrims even smaller.

For an instant, Lan debated dropping from his vantage point, getting onto the creature's back, and trying to find a soft spot in the thick armor. Between head and abdomen gave the best chance of stopping the scorpion. Then he saw the stinger arc over, aiming for the spider. Krek danced away—barely.

Lan Martak knew it was impossible to attack the scorpion by straddling its back. That tail would slice him in two. He kept climbing.

What seemed years later, he pulled himself onto the top of the cliff, bruised, bloodied, and out of the breath. Again he looked down, from more than forty feet up this time. Krek's hunting web gleamed in the sunlight. The scorpion's hard shell looked like burnished brass. And, over the sounds of the battling arachnids, came the steady, doleful chanting from Ehznoll's people. Less than twenty feet from the titanic battle, they continued to pray.

Lan intended to do more than pray.

He used his sword. Thrusting it between two large boulders, he levered and bent his back. Hands slipping from the blood, muscles aching from exertion, lungs burning, sweat running into eyes and mouth, he pulled. Nothing happened at first, then he heard a deep-throated creaking.

"Please, don't let the sword break," he moaned as he redoubled his efforts. A deeper creaking noise echoed down the valley. Then he fell heavily, the boulder pulled from its place.

He rolled over and called to those below, "Watch out!" But his words came too late for any to react.

They were saved by the scorpion's lightning-fast reflexes. It saw the boulder hurtling downward at it. The long, deadly tail struck out with force, but it only served to deflect the rock from its trajectory. It fell onto the back of the scorpion. A sound like a pistol shot rang out as the heavy rock crushed the monster to a bloody, ichorous pulp.

Lan felt his gorge rising at the sight, but he controlled himself. Weakly, he swallowed, tasting bitterness. He spat and that helped. By the time he began his descent back to Krek and Ehznoll and the others, he'd regained his composure.

"I swear I saw someone from up there, Krek. I wasn't hallucinating."

"Who else wanders these hills? Only Ehznoll and his pilgrims, friend Lan Martak. No one else on this world would be so intent on discovering paradise."

"I saw someone," the man said firmly. "Only one man, leading a pack animal. Might have been three miles up the canyon, but certainly no farther."

"I feel no one," said the spider.

"You're still shaking from the fight with the scorpion."

"Nonsense." The spider shook even harder.

"And those crazy bastards didn't even lift a hand to help," snapped Lan, anger replacing the fright he'd felt anew seeing the crushed carcass of the monstrous scorpion.

"Are you referring to my band?" said Ehznoll. "We destroyed the creature. What more can you ask of us?"

"You did what?" roared Lan, losing his temper.

"Our prayers were answered by the godhead residing in the planet."

"No godhead climbed that cliff. No godhead pried loose that boulder. *I* did it all. Me!"

"Without the sweet earth's approval, you could have done nothing. I told you the earth wouldn't allow us to die in plain sight of the sky. The truly devout die only out of sight of the infinite, awful void."

"He does seem to have a point, friend Lan Martak."

"What?" Lan spun on his friend, then quieted. In a voice as low and controlled as he could make it, he said, "Didn't your hunting strands hold the scorpion down?"

"Of course, but they were anchored in the earth."

"See?" said Ehznoll, his eyes gleaming with religious fervor.

"You're not becoming a convert, are you, Krek?"

"We accept all into the faith." Ehznoll tossed dirt onto Krek's furry legs. The spider danced away. "Accept our sacrament. Join us in our ecstasy!"

"I will consider it," said Krek, warily watching the pilgrim for more fountains of dust.

"Be like the clods of the earth. Join with your neighbors. Unite into a whole."

"Let's just be on our way," Lan said tiredly. He ached and his horse had been slaughtered. From now on he walked with the rest of them. While Ehznoll went back to his band, Lan sank down and closed his eyes. Visions appeared immediately. He fought down panic at the sight of a fleshless skull floating, seeming to mock him.

His eyelids flickered up. Krek stood over him.

"I felt his power, too. Claybore is near."

"Then he doesn't have the Kinetic Sphere. Not yet!"

"It is a long ways to the summit of Mount Tartanius. We have much to contend with."

"What?" asked Lan. "You don't like our travelling companions? You're not going to join them in a nice dirt bath?" The sight of the spider shuddering gave Lan the revenge he needed.

"The thought of dust eternally on my legs is worse than burning off the fur. Poof! I would ignite like a torch. A flambeau blazing throughout the night, my screams meaning nothing. Oh, woe, how can I ever avoid the dangers of this life?"

"You're doing a good enough job, old spider. We make quite a team."

"We do, at that," Krek said, his mood changing in a mercurial fashion peculiar to him. They walked past the crushed scorpion once more. "For a fellow arachnid, he possessed limited wit. Why, he refused to even speak to me."

"It talked?"

"No, but I can; therefore he must have similar powers."

"Different worlds, different creatures."

"Humph," snorted the spider. "You humans are pervasive, one might even say pernicious. I descern no difference between your species on one world or the next."

Lan saw no point in arguing. He had no explanations. What Krek said was true. On the worlds they'd travelled so far, humans had been native to each. Perhaps human cenotaphs opened only onto human worlds. If that were true, the Kinetic Sphere might lead to worlds without any men at all. Entire worlds populated with alien beings beckoned to Lan.

First, he had to recover the Sphere.

"Do you think it was just another pilgrim I saw?"

"What other pilgrim?"

"The one I saw from the cliff. I told you not ten minutes ago."

"I sense no one ahead of us. Why has there been no evidence of passage, if you did see a man with a pack animal?"

"These canyons intersect. He might have come up another one, one leading into this from an angle."

"You invent people to take your mind off our odious companions."

"You might be right in other circumstances, but I *saw* someone ahead of us. I . . . I can't explain why I feel that's so important. We're out in the middle of nowhere. Why should there be so many people crowding into this one small area?"

"Mere pilgrims. Others like Ehznoll seek the wisdom of the crags. Perhaps they even wish to swing free, from peak to peak, savoring the freedom of a web. Who am I to say? I am a nothing, a poor beast beset by others of my class, an outcast good only for slaughtering weakling humans."

"Weakling humans?" protested Lan. "Who actually killed the scorpion?"

"I allow myself to be enticed away from web and my dear Klawn, to walk the Cenotaph Road and humiliate myself constantly. Oh, woe, I am nothing, nothing!"

The spider crouched down and melted into the shadows cast by the ravine wall. His eyes welled over with tears, which fell to dampen the dry sand of the arroyo floor.

"Come on, Krek, it's not that bad. You're just feeling sorry for yourself. We'll get to the top of Mount Tartanius, get back the Kinetic Sphere, and find Inyx. Wouldn't you like to see her again? The two of you hit it off so well, I'd think you'd do anything to see her again."

"Inyx?"

"Inyx," said Lan firmly. He'd learned ways of motivating the spider when depression hit. Inyx was one.

"We should try, I suppose." The spider rose up and began walking on unsteady legs. Lan watched in concern. The battle with the scorpion had taken much out of the spider. He had no idea what energy it took to spin webs; it had to require considerable effort. Krek had spun almost a mile of web in a very short time. He deserved pampering—for a while.

"Rejoice!" came Ehznoll's shrill voice. "The earth loves us. We are a part of the mighty soil."

Lan shook his head. Putting up with the pilgrims might be more difficult than fending off all the grey-clad soldiers on the planet, even including the hate-driven Kiska k'Adesina. He might have made a bad mistake in not eliminating her, but cold-blooded killing didn't suit him. At least, she and the others in her tiny band hadn't tracked him down yet. With any luck, he'd be atop the mountain, in possession of the Sphere, reunited with Inyx, and on his way to permanently stopping Claybore before any of the greys caught up. He walked on, then stopped and looked back. Krek had frozen, eyes wide in horror.

"Krek, another scorpion?" Visions of a nest of the twelve-foot monsters flashed through his mind. He barely heard the choked reply.

"Water. Coming down the canyon. We'll all drown!"

The spider shot forth a long strand of climbing web and vanished up the face of the cliff that had taken Lan long minutes to scale.

"Krek, come down here. There's nothing to—"

Lan Martak felt the earth shuddering beneath his boot soles, shuddering as if a tidal wave thundered down upon him.

CHAPTER NINE

"Krek, don't!" screamed Lan. The spider bounded away, bouncing once or twice off the face of the cliff, climbing swiftly, leaving Lan and the other humans behind to face their deaths.

The rumbling grew greater, deeper, more powerful. Lan glanced from side to side, estimating his chances. A wall of water coming down from high in the mountains would easily fill this ravine. Merely getting up on the slopes of the arroyo wouldn't help much if the flash flood proved too large.

"Krek, use your web to save us!"

The spider's bulk diminished as he scuttled over the top of the cliff. Lan saw his friend shiver and shake in fear. The only thing the arachnid feared more than fire was water. Lan took no time to berate Krek for his cowardice. Much had happened to the spider to shake what little self-confidence he had. He had to move quickly. Saving his own life took precedence.

"Up the slopes. Hurry. Flood!" he cried to the pilgrims. They stared at him, eyes wide, expressions blank. They were so lost in their religious ceremonies that they hadn't felt the vibrations beneath their feet—or if they had, they thought their earth god answered their supplications.

Lan rushed forward, using the flat of his sword to smack bottoms and chivvy along the pilgrims. They moved—too slowly.

The entire planet shook under Lan's feet. A quick look up the ravine made him shake as hard as Krek had. A grey-green wall of water forty feet high smashed its way down, ripping out dead trees, picking up boulders five feet in diameter, promising sudden death. Lan forgot about the pilgrims; his own life hung in the balance. He scrambled up the side of the sandy embankment, fingers clawing frantically.

The first rush of the water ripped him loose from his precarious hold. Flung outward, he smashed painfully into a rock. As agonizing as this was, it saved his life. The powerful current carried him around the rock and up against earth. The pounding of water against his body wedged him further and further into the crevice between rock and dirt. Gasping, sputtering, he fought weakly against the water.

He survived. That thought went over and over in his head. He struggled harder and pulled himself up onto the rock that had saved his life. The man looked downriver at the watery maelstrom boiling around the site of the battle with the scorpion. Neither the carcass nor the boulder that had crushed the life from it remained.

If he'd been swept into the raging river, no amount of swimming ability could have saved him.

He turned, slipped, caught himself, then more carefully sat on the rock and peered upstream. Tiny water droplets exploded into the air, caught the sun, and turned into colorful prisms splitting the sun's rays. Even in destruction came beauty. The awesome tide abated but little. Lan Martak peered at the banks, seeking some sign of life, some indication that Ehznoll and the others had lived.

Nothing.

"Ehznoll!" he cried out. His words were sucked under by the roaring waters just a few feet away. "Ehznoll!" he called again. "Where are you?"

A tiny murmur, hardly more than a subliminal

message, reached his ears. The singsong chant built in tempo and volume until he recognized the words.

"Ehznoll!"

The chant came still louder. The fanatical pilgrim recited his prayers. He'd survived the onslaught of water.

Then Lan saw another survivor: Melira. But from the way she clung desperately to the rock in the center of the river, he could see that her strength would soon vanish and she'd be swept away.

"Melira, are you hurt?"

"The good earth will protect me," she called back. Her voice started out strong enough, then weakened. "Water is a part of the earth. The soil sucks it up, embraces it to its bosom. I shall join the water."

"Don't let loose. I'll save you!"

How he'd perform this miracle feat, Lan didn't know. The first thing he did was strip off his heavy sword belt. His boots and tunic followed. Only then did he study the expanse he had to cross to save the woman. The floodwaters had receded slightly, but not enough to aid him. There wasn't any way a human could swim that torrential outpouring from high on the mountain.

"Friend Lan Martak, I am so pitiable. A coward, not only to my own kind, but to humans, as well. How can I ever redeem myself?" The words came amid tiny chokes and moans of emotional pain. Lan looked over to the top of the cliff, barely ten feet above him now because of the water. Krek cowered there, trembling, his head hanging over the precipice while the bulk of his body remained safely on solid rock.

"Spin a web. Hurry, Krek. Let me swing out to the middle of the river. Melira." He pointed. The spider bobbed his head, then emitted a spitting noise. A long, slender strand whirled down to *splat!* on the rock beside the man.

Lan looked at it with trepidation. The web-stuff's diameter was hardly more than a single sewing thread's. He tested it and worried even more. The elasticity of this silk might drop him into the drink. Still, Lan had no other choice but to trust the spider's spinning skills. Melira weakened visibly, her fingers turning white against the rock, slowly slipping, letting her body be whipped about by the current.

Lan Martak took a deep breath, gripped the thread, then stepped out over the river.

"Noooo!" he shrieked as the thread lengthened under his weight.

Just as the man was positive he'd be dropped into the river and swept away, he snapped hard and swung past Melira. The web-stuff had stretched as much as it could and now held his weight easily. But he'd gone past the woman and crashed into the side of the cliff. Getting back to her might prove difficult.

"Allow me to aid you," came the spider's voice from above.

The thread jiggled and bounced, then began pulling Lan upward. When he reached an out-jutting, Krek stopped.

"Swing free now. It is simple enough for even a hatchling."

"Here goes nothing." Lan again stepped into nothingness. This time, however, he aimed more carefully. As the short arc swept him by the failing Melira, he reached down with one arm and caught her about the waist.

Accomplishing this made his hand slip on the thread. It was too thin for an easy grasp.

"Krek, I'm slipping, I . . . I can't hold both her and myself."

The spider didn't answer with words. A tiny drop of amber fluid dripped slowly down the length of the taut web material. Lan held on the best he could to keep Melira from flying away in the current. His arms aching from the strain, his hand cramping and ready to release and throw both of them into the water to drown, the man wondered why his life should end in this fashion.

The droplet touched his skin. He shrieked in pain and involuntarily tried to pull back, to let loose of the web-thread. His hand glued firmly to the line.

Slowly, one inch at a time, he felt himself rising. He tightened his grip around the now-unconscious woman's waist. The effort made his shoulders ache even more. Muscle strain and sudden spasms caused his right hand to open on the thread; the spider glue held him firmly. Seeing this, Lan concentrated all his effort on holding the woman. To drop her now after rescuing her would be worse than never reaching her at all.

"There," he finally heard the spider say. "You are safe. Now you may berate me, denigrate my abilities, call me craven."

"Krek," Lan cried, throwing his arms around the spider's bulky abdomen, "thank you!"

"He thanks me," the spider sighed. Tears formed in the dish-shaped chocolate eyes. "I show my true colors and he thanks me. I am a coward, friend Lan Martak—no, not friend. I dare not call anyone my friend. Who would have me?"

"I will, you crazy eight-legged fool. You saved me—both of us."

Melira stirred on the ground, still unconscious.

"I allowed you to be placed in the danger."

"Krek," Lan said seriously, seeing the spider needed consoling, "bravery isn't doing daring acts. Bravery is overcoming your fear. You were frightened and yet you overcame your fear of the water enough to rescue both me and the pilgrim."

"You think me brave?"

"I do."

"Humans are most peculiar." With that Krek trotted over to the now-stirring woman. He poked at her with one taloned claw. "She needs some attention. Perhaps you should perform some of those human mating rituals now."

"I think not." Lan knelt beside the woman, now sputtering to get fluid out of her lungs. She turned onto her side, coughed, and finally began breathing normally. Her eyes opened, stared up an Lan.

"Y-you saved me."

"Krek helped."

"Why?"

"Couldn't just let you die, could I?"

Melira sobbed as Lan held her. He found this chore less tiresome than it might have been earlier. The water had washed away most of the dirt in her hair and on her body. While she wasn't totally clean, she'd been improved by the ordeal.

"I . . . I cannot thank you. The good earth must do that." She turned wide eyes up to Lan's. He felt a surge of discomfort.

"Better check to see how the others in your party fared."

"Yes," she said, the moment gone. "I hear the earth chants being sung. Ehznoll survived."

Lan helped her to her feet. The three started the long, arduous climb down the far side of the cliff, skirting the deadly waters to find a handful of survivors gathered around their leader.

"Their deaths were *good*," insisted Ehznoll. He leaned forward and thumped a fist into hard ground. "They were swallowed up by the waters, and the waters soaked into the earth. They returned to the bosom of dirt from which we all sprang."

"No death's a good one," said Lan glumly. After rejoining Ehznoll and the four others who had escaped the floodwaters, they'd walked along the rim of the canyon, heading upward into the mountains. Less than an hour's travel had brought them to an earthen dam intended to hold back the water. "Especially when it is deliberate."

"How can you say that? The earth barrier gave way. The earth *wanted* to receive our pilgrims. Their destiny wasn't atop Mount Tartanius. It was here, going into the earth."

"Someone ripped open the dam and tried to drown us," said Lan. He pointed out the clear indications of the attempted murder. Sheer, mirror-smooth sides remained above the water, showing where incredible forces had been unleashed. The dirt itself had fused into a glassy substance that broke under Lan's knife point.

"The god of earth did it in his . . . new form." Ehznoll's voice softened and he dropped into tones reserved for his more reverent moments. "I *saw* him. The new god."

"You're saying your god sliced through the earth like that?" A large chunk of the vitrified dam came loose and tumbled into the still-raging water. The green, turbulent water swallowed the material as if it were only an appetizer before a larger meal.

"Yes." Ehznoll's voice lowered even more. "I *saw*! He was as our god of the earth: disembodied. Only his intelligence floated."

"What?"

"His head floated. He nodded toward me and eyes flashed. He is a new god on earth. And we are privileged to be here at his assumption of power."

Lan Martak scowled, then glanced over at Krek. The spider appeared not to be listening. The arachnid had been lost in his own thoughts since they'd rejoined Ehznoll's band. The description Ehznoll gave of his new god worried Lan more than Krek's depression.

"This new god's eyes," he pressed. "Did ruby beams shoot from them?"

"No."

Lan let out a lungful of air he hadn't known he held.

"The beams were crimson."

"Claybore!"

Ehznoll stared at the man.

"You know of him? That's his name? Our god of the earth is nameless, omnipresent, needing no human term. But this new god is compact, condensed, a living relic. Even his name speaks of the earth."

The pilgrim gripped Lan's arm with steely fingers. Lan pulled free and sat back on his heels, looking from Ehznoll to Melira to the other four. The zealots accepted every word Ehznoll uttered as gospel. He talked them into believing Claybore was a god.

"I've heard of this Claybore, nothing more," Lan said carefully. The man feared Krek would contradict him, but the spider remained wrapped in the dark cloak of his own thoughts and feelings.

"Our tenets change. This new god—Claybore! —works wonders on our earth, for us, through us, because of us. He split this dam to carry eighteen of our order to their justly deserved graves."

"Surrounded by dirt," chimed in Melira and the others.

"One with dirt," Ehznoll answered ritualistically. They crossed their wrists and dropped into a kneeling pose, eyes afire with religious fervor. Lan left them to go study the edge of the dam more closely.

Glass. It sloped down five feet and then vanished into green, swiftly flowing waters. Claybore had used a spell to slash through the retaining dam and send a wall of water down the canyon. That much was clear. But who aided the decapitated mage? Who acted as his legs? Lan felt sure now that he had seen a man with a pack animal. That man carried along the wooden box containing the sorcerer's skull. Without the Kinetic Sphere, Claybore lacked mobility.

In a way, he felt happy this had happened. Claybore feared him, feared his ability to reach the top of Mount Tartanius first. Knowing that a foe as worthy as Claybore felt this way added spring to Lan's step, energy to his body, determination to his quest.

"Come along, old spider," he said, kicking Krek in the ribs. "Time to be walking. We've got a race on our hands, and Claybore's only a few miles ahead of us."

Krek lumbered to his feet and began working his way upslope. Lan followed, with Ehznoll's band behind.

Mount Tartanius towered in front of them. For three days they'd fought their way ever higher in the foothills of the Sulliman Range. Now only the soaring peak itself remained between them and its summit.

"I can 'see' it," said Krek, speaking his first words in almost two days. "It radiates immense power."

"I sense it, too," said Lan. He closed his eyes. Floating in front of him was a brilliantly glowing ball of incandescent gas. It spun and turned and twisted, leaving misty strands of itself behind. He had no idea what this image meant; the Kinetic Sphere was solid. No doubt remained in his mind, though, that he now shared Krek's vision of the gateway between worlds.

"There is also evidence of those who passed this way before us."

"What? Where?"

He knelt down to peer more intently at the hard, flintlike rock. Tiny scratches showed where a shod horse had trodden recently. The weather had yet to round off the edges of the scratch marks, to fill the grooves with dirt. The track led directly forward toward Mount Tartanius.

"I cannot sense Claybore, however," finished the spider.

"Nor I," said Lan. "I've been straining my magic-sensing ability to the utmost, but either he hasn't used any spells or they are so devious I'm not able to detect them."

"His powers are diminished by separation from the Kinetic Sphere," said Krek. "His spells might be of such low-grade power they remain below your threshold of sensing."

"Our new god came this way? You are mages? You're sure?" cut in Melira. "Ehznoll! They say our new god has come this way. Recently!"

"Glory be to the top of Mount Tartanius!" shrieked Ehznoll. "I knew we did well allowing you to join our pilgrimage."

The six earth-lovers dropped to pray. Lan shook his head sadly. The cleaning from the inadvertent baths they'd all been subjected to hadn't lasted long. The very first day on the trail away from the dam, Ehznoll and the others had taken to rolling in the dust, patting it into one another's skin, matting their hair until it hung in greasy ropes. Melira, possibly out of deference to Lan's sensibilities, hadn't become quite as filthy as she'd been before. The difference between her state now and then was one of degree only.

Lan cringed whenever he saw her eyeing him.

He turned to Krek, saying, "How are you faring? I find myself increasingly winded."

"The air is fine. In the Egrii Mountains, we spiders inhabit peaks much higher than this lowly pass."

"Lowly for you, high for me. I'm used to sea level. Aren't you the least bit tired?"

"No."

As they moved on after Ehznoll had finished his new supplications, Lan wondered how much longer he could keep up the pace. The pilgrims were fired with religious ecstasy. Sheer enthusiasm kept them going forward. Krek had been born and raised at elevations much greater. His own lungs burned with every breath. He forced himself to suck in as much air as possible, hold it longer than usual, then exhale quickly. Even this didn't supply his aching muscles the oxygen necessary for quick pace.

"There's a hut," he panted. "Let's rest there."

"As you wish, friend Lan Martak," agreed the spider. His mood lightened appreciably as they worked ever higher. He returned to the lands he knew best and slowly forgot his lapse of bravery when the dam had been sundered. "This rude peasant hut is old but serviceable for one of your species. If I understand the workings, the pipe emerging from the roof might be connected to a heating device inside."

Lan rubbed chapped hands together and felt a brief surge of warmth from the friction. To sit in front of a wood-fired stove seemed closer to heaven to him than the crest of Mount Tartanius.

"Come on. I'll bet the last party's even left us firewood."

"The last party is likely to have been Claybore and his lackey," pointed out the spider. That dampened Lan's spirit and made him more cautious. While Ehznoll and the others collapsed to pray loudly after hearing Claybore's name again, Lan circled the hut, critically studying it.

"I don't see any traps. I don't sense any magical ward spells. Anything, Krek?"

The spider's head swayed from side to side, indicating he "saw" nothing.

"Here goes nothing." Lan kicked open the door and stood, sword in hand, waiting. No demons raved outward to devour him. No spells turned him into a newt. Only the musty odor of a long-closed room came forth to make his nostrils twitch.

He entered. The hut remained as it had been for decades. Piles of equipment left by prior expeditions littered the floor. Heavy furs dangled from pegs on the walls. The pot-bellied stove itself dominated the center of the room. Lan couldn't imagine the work it'd taken to get such a heavy iron implement up the slopes to this point.

"Firewood," said Krek, disdain in his voice. "And do not light the fire while I am within spark distance. A tiny ember might ignite my fur." Ripples passed up and down the legs.

"Don't worry, old spider. I'll only use a small pyromancy spell. And it'll be inside the stove." Lan poked about the litter and found a grimy fur cloak long enough to barely drag the ground when he slung it about his shoulders. "This is going to be a great help. The nights are too cold for the clothing we have. There's enough here to keep us from freezing to death."

"Speak for yourself. The weather is fine."

Lan ignored him and dug further. He touched a small wooden crate and felt electric tingles pass up his arm. Magic. He cautiously opened the lid and saw a dozen woollen caps inside, caps to be pulled down over the head with eyeholes and no other opening.

"Guess we're not supposed to talk or breathe," he said. The feel of magic still persisted. He didn't detect any hint of evil, only magic. He shoved his head into one of the caps, positioning the eyes so he could see. "I can breathe!" he exclaimed. "The magic spell does something to make breathing easier."

"Your voice remains muffled," said Krek. The thick wool prevented Lan from hearing the softer "Good."

"And foodstuffs. Trail rations. Enough for us to make a good try at the mountain."

"Enough for all you humans. This spot is obviously popular with those scaling mountains. It is a shame you cannot leave behind for future travellers the masks and fur capes when you no longer require them."

It was true. No matter what the outcome atop Mount Tartanius, Lan Martak would never again pass this way. If he regained the Kinetic Sphere, that magical gateway opened a myriad worlds to him; he wouldn't risk the descent to return this equipment. And if Claybore triumphed, Lan needed nothing at all—except the dirt around him that Ehznoll and the others worshipped.

Lan didn't seek a grave. He sought Inyx—and freedom to walk the Cenotaph Road.

CHAPTER TEN

"Look out!"

Lan Martak ducked, bent forward, and felt heavy rock cascade onto the pack he carried. His legs buckled and he teetered on the ledge, his fingers beginning to slip from the tenuous hold on loose stone. A strong hand pushed him back against the sheer rock face of the cliff.

"Thanks, Ehznoll," he said, his breath coming in short, quick pants in spite of the magical breathing device he wore. "I'd've tumbled over the edge."

"No, you wouldn't," the pilgrim said firmly. "The good earth does not want you. Not yet. You have to fulfill your mission first."

Lan glanced down. The ledge they traversed was hardly wider than his boots; the drop beyond that six-inch width looked like miles. The valley so far below glowed a living green, distance fogging it over with a soft purple. He closed his eyes and turned to face the cliff. The journey was easier when he looked inward.

"What mission?" he asked the fanatical pilgrim. "Getting off this ledge alive?"

"Meeting once again with the new god."

"Claybore."

"Claybore," the man affirmed. "You must be privileged beyond most mortals to have met him."

"What if I told you he wasn't a god, but a devil? A demon sent to confound you and steer you away from righteousness?"

Ehznoll laughed.

"I've seen visions of Claybore. The good earth has spoken to me. He is a new god, and no blasphemy you utter changes that. Or do you only test me? Yes, that's it. You think to test my faith. No, fellow pilgrim, my faith is unshakable."

Lan swallowed hard as he inched across the ledge and found an open area in the side of the mountain. Mount Tartanius abounded with such refuges, for which he was dutifully thankful. He worried over Ehznoll's single-minded belief that the vision he'd seen constituted godhood for the decapitated sorceror. No amount of argument convinced Ehznoll that Claybore had tried to kill them. The man's entire life had been geared to religious beliefs; when his first "vision" came, he misinterpreted it totally.

Lan had seen Claybore. The magics used by the sorcerer projected images, nightmares, that could be seen as clearly as Nashira's magic eyes had watched Lan back in Melitarsus. Lan recognized the visions for what they were. Ehznoll, in his haste to believe, erred. Mistaking evil for good had been done before Ehznoll. It would be done again by a myriad others, after this lapse of skepticism proved his undoing.

"Hello, friend Lan Martak," came Krek's voice. The spider walked down the side of a rock and crouched beside him. "Enjoy your jaunt along the mountain face?"

"Loved it," Lan lied. The arachnid cantered off to let the humans make their own way. Lan didn't doubt Krek's abilities could take him to the summit in only a few days. Only friendship and the need for companionship kept the spider from racing ahead.

"These smaller lumps give way to real hills farther in."

Lan glanced nervously down the sheer face of the mountain. A mile, maybe two, of empty space before the green valley amounted to more than "small lumps" in his opinion.

"The way is easy for several miles. This crevice broadens, goes inward, and provides a nice path even a cripple can navigate," the spider went on. "Even a human cripple," he added in a smug, superior tone.

"Any sign of Claybore?" Lan asked in a soft voice. He didn't want to stir Ehznoll again.

"None. The man carrying the wooden case containing the skull is not to be seen, either. Most mysterious. I doubt any but a spider is able to scale Mount Tartanius so quickly. I am at a loss to explain it."

"Maybe he knows a secret way up."

"If so, he will arrive at the crest before us."

"Tell me something cheerful."

"There is another party of humans ahead."

"What? Who? Why didn't you mention this before?"

"I commented first on Claybore, as you requested. Then I proceeded to report on the man thought to be supplying transport to the skull. I now arrive at the news of another party of five humans, less than a mile distant. They struggle along, one of their number being very old and infirm."

"Five of them. Could one of those five be Claybore's legs?"

"Doubtful."

"Why?"

"None has a pack animal with him."

"But, Krek," moaned Lan, "look at the slopes we've been climbing. No pack animal can make it along those ledges. He'd've left it behind. He would be walking, just like I am."

"You walk because the scorpion killed your horse."

"I . . . never mind." Lan shook his head. The spider's logic—or lack of it—defied analysis. Because the man aiding Claybore had a pack animal once, he had to have it now, or so thought Krek. The terrain proved too treacherous for any but the most agile now. Something in Krek's mind didn't make the jump that any pack creature remained behind.

"Shall I ask those ahead to slow so we can join them?"

"Let's approach them cautiously. If they're only another group of earth lovers, Ehznoll will be happy.

For my part, I'm not so sure if I can handle more than a handful of them at a time."

Ehznoll, Melira, and the other four performed their noonday prayer service, kneeling and rubbing what little dirt they found over one another. Lan wondered if he ever wanted to meet others of this sect, especially now. He had no clear feeling for Ehznoll's position in the earth church. If Ehznoll proved to be an important figure venerated by others, his estimation of Claybore's godhood boded ill. On the other hand, Lan might approve of a divergent sect challenging Ehznoll's devout belief in the new god.

"Let's catch up with them as soon as we can."

"By nightfall," Krek assured him.

Hard walking over loose stone brought them ever closer to the other group throughout the afternoon. Lan knew the others had sighted them. From their attitude, it mattered little whether Lan, Krek, Ehznoll, and the others overtook them or not. They kept moving at their slow, deliberate pace, neither stopping nor speeding up. Just as the sun set in the west, casting bloody light over a small mesa, the two groups met for the first time.

"Greetings," called Lan to the old man who appeared to be in charge. "We're pilgrims. Scaling Mount Tartanius."

"Good thing you don't think you're swimming a damn ocean, then," the old man said sarcastically. One clear eye surveyed Lan critically. "They look like pilgrims. You don't."

"Oh, but I am. We climb Mount Tartanius to worship the earth's attempt to gut the sky."

"Earth worshippers, eh?"

"Yes."

"And the arachnid?" the old man asked. Lan scowled slightly. Krek had remained back, out of sight, as they closed with this group. Creatures of his size only brought unwanted and unwarranted response. If the scorpion proved any indication, arachnids might be very unpopular in this locale. Even worse, he felt as if gossamer wings brushed his mind: magic use.

Lan looked at the old man more carefully. No doubt remained in his mind that the man questioning him created the spells he sensed. Tiny twitches of the lips betrayed continual mutterings. The old man used a scrying spell to find Krek.

"Krek stays out of sight—to avoid unwanted fright on the part of less enlightened men."

The old man smiled, yellowed teeth showing between his chapped lips. A scraggly white beard had frosted from his breath and the cold, and the few wisps of hair on the top of his head lay in a tangled mat. Deep furrows ran over the face, indicating more years than Lan cared to guess at. The rest of the man's body was hidden by thick, ankle-length brown and green robes and heavy mittens.

"You know."

"Isn't it obvious?" said Lan, more boldly now. "You're having no trouble breathing. You don't wear any sort of apparatus or spell-driven mask. I'm young, in trim, and I still gasp. You unerringly located Krek. Need I go on? You are a sorcerer."

"I make a pilgrimage. To the summit."

"For what purpose?"

"Don't question me, youngling," the man snapped. His brief good mood evaporated as quickly as fog in the hot morning sun. "My business is my own."

"I'm sure," said Lan. "At least allow me to introduce the others in my party." He went around the small circle, starting with Ehznoll and finishing with Krek, now come from behind a large rock. "And you are?" Lan probed, fishing for an answer.

"I told you. A pilgrim."

"Then you are as we," said Ehznoll, his eyes

glowing. "We can combine forces, share services. My friends and I were readying evening prayers. Come, join us in praying to the generous earth."

"Fall off the mountain," the old man said bitterly. "I need none of you. Be on your way. Leave me alone."

"We camp here for the night," said Lan. "If you don't like it, then you can leave. But we stay *here*." The firmness in the young adventurer's voice caused the old man to stop and glare.

"I am Abasi-Abi."

"Well, Abasi-Abi, welcome. If you and your party wish to share our meager rations . . ." Lan left the invitation dangling. Abasi-Abi spun and stalked off, his stride springy for one so old.

"You humans fluctuate in mood so," commented Krek. "Some are overly friendly. Take Melira, for instance. She certainly desires an opportunity to engage you in your curious mating rituals. This Abasi-Abi, on the other side of the web, is quite surly."

"And I suppose spiders don't have such wide variations in attitude."

"No. Either we view one another as food, or not. Mostly we exist high in our webs, swinging, swaying, revelling in the ways of nature. Interaction is held to a minimum. For which I am glad. If we arachnids ever came into closer contact, why, we might begin acting like you humans."

"A tragedy," Lan said sarcastically.

"Yes," agreed Krek. Again, sarcasm had been wasted.

Lan Martak turned away from Abasi-Abi, saying to Krek, "Let's prepare some food while Ehznoll and his disciples toss dirt on one another. I'm hungry."

He'd taken only a few steps when he staggered, fell to his knees, and held his head in cupped hands. If a berserk woodsman had taken an ax to his head, the pain wouldn't have been much different. His eyes closed, the pain building in a sawtoothed wave that threatened to drive him crazy, Lan "saw" Claybore.

The fleshless skull floated a few inches in front of him, the ruby beams from the eyesockets lashing out in a slow motion that allowed him ample time to feel fear surge inside. The ends of the ruby lances came closer, closer, ever closer. He tried to dodge. He was frozen to the spot. Lan knew that if those beams touched him, he died. Helplessly, he watched the inexorable advance of death.

A new element entered the nightmare vision. A presence, a force, came from behind him, welled up from within. The ruby gaze from Claybore's skull still inched forward, but the beams bent, curved away, and passed harmlessly to either side of Lan's body. The sorcerer's skull turned in mid-air, jaws clacking ominously.

As suddenly as the force had paralyzed him, it vanished. Lan groaned and fell face down onto the hard rock. He was aware of Krek standing over him, guarding him, trying to figure out what new malady assailed his fragile human friend.

Lan pushed his way up to hands and knees. He felt as if his innards had turned to molasses. Shaking in reaction, he turned over painfully and sat upright.

"Friend Lan Martak, are you all right?"

"No," he said. "Yes. I don't know."

"Magic?"

"You sensed it, then." Lan knew that the spider's ability to sense the cenotaphs was more acute than any magical gift he possessed; that sensing of cenotaphs had to be only the edge of a more developed magical talent.

"I did. The sensation was not unlike walls closing in all around. I felt as if I might be crushed. No specific threat posed itself, yet I tensed in fear. Never have I felt so weak, so miserable, not even when forced to slay in the arenas of the Suzerain of Melitarsus. How is it I left my web in the Egrii Mountains? How, how, how? Oh, woe!"

"Krek, calm down. Everything's all right now. The spells have passed. I wonder if I don't owe our new friend a little thanks for saving me from Claybore." He looked across the rocky flat to Abasi-Abi's camp. The self-proclaimed sorcerer hunched over near a fire, head down, appearing little more than a grey lump in the evening shadows. The sun set rapidly and the blood-red cast turned to thick blackness.

"The winds of magic blow strongly about this peak," said Krek.

"I couldn't agree more," said Lan, finally getting a measure of strength back. "And I fear this is only the opening round of a more deadly battle."

He and the spider joined Ehznoll in a meager, tasteless dinner.

"Mount Tartanius is not easily scaled," said Lan. "Look at that traverse. It requires the entire party to be roped together. If one slips, then the others on either side can prevent tragedy. Even then, it'll take hours to cross."

Abasi-Abi frowned. His eyes darted across the indicated area of mountain, then downward to the slope where they currently rested. He worked it out in his own mind whether or not Lan's approach merited more than sarcastic dismissal.

"We can make it without such precautions."

"Try it and your guides will be dead. Are they so inexperienced?"

"Are you so knowledgeable?" shot back the sorcerer. Lan felt a sharp pain in his chest, along with the bright glow of magic. As the man spoke, he uttered spells. His anger had overflowed and allowed a spell to be directed against Lan. Lan began muttering counter spells of his own. The pain slowly went away. The sorcerer's eyes widened slightly in disbelief, but he made no comment about the protective spells.

"Yes," Lan said firmly. "I've spent much time on my home world climbing mountains. In the el-Liot Mountains I've scaled all but the highest."

"Were any like this peak?"

"I've never seen a mountain this large," admitted Lan. "But the techniques used for smaller expeditions are the same. Separately, neither of our parties will reach the summit. Together, we stand a chance. A slim one, considering the dangers, but a chance."

"What do you know of the dangers?" Abasi-Abi paced to and fro, hands locked behind his back, head down.

"Dangers?" called out Ehznoll. "There are none. The sweet earth prevents harm from coming to us. And our new god is atop the mountain, waiting for us."

Lan glanced from the pilgrim to Abasi-Abi. The sorcerer didn't inquire as to the identity of this "new god." Either he cared little about the earth religion or he knew that Ehznoll spoke of Claybore. Lan Martak couldn't decide which it was. The potent magics being tossed back and forth had continued throughout the night. He knew he sensed only the fringes of that magic; a duel of titanic proportions built.

"Is your reason for scaling the peak worth the risk?" asked Lan of the sorcerer.

"We all ascend for valid reasons."

Lan didn't press the issue. Abasi-Abi was hardly a likeable man, and his occasional fits of ire might prove deadly. Lan rubbed the spot on his chest where the magical bolt had hit. While the skin remained unblemished, the innards felt as if he'd been burned. If his own reasons for climbing Mount Tartanius hadn't been so overwhelming, Lan knew he'd turn around and leave this very instant. He climbed with a religious fanatic and a sorcerer whose anger might kill; he climbed to a summit impossibly high and fought Claybore along the way.

Lan Martak shook his head. Life wasn't easy. Certainly not as easy as dying.

"An ice field," he called back to Ehznoll, roped just behind him. "I think it's safe." Lan used the tip of his sword to test the frozen terrain. This miniature glacier had rushed out of a high canyon in the side of Mount Tartanius, then had been covered with a thin, bright glaze of half-frozen snow. The surface crunched under his boots as he tested each step.

"Push on, you fool. We are exposed here. The wind comes off the mountain." Abasi-Abi's snarling voice reached him and made him mad. All day long they'd climbed difficult slopes. Simply because this ice flow appeared level and safe didn't make it either. Just as Lan started to tell the complaining sorcerer this, he stepped down into . . . nothing.

"Aieee!"

He fell only five feet before the rope jerked him to a halt. But the precipitous fall had caused Ehznoll to lose his balance. Lan felt himself slipping lower and lower. The pilgrim appeared at the lip of the crevice, then came tumbling over, too.

"Ehznoll, are the others holding us?" he called up.

The man above him struggled for a grip on the slick, cold surface. Only after finding a tiny ledge did he answer.

"I think so. We saw you go. I didn't have time to brace myself, but Abasi-Abi did. I think."

Lan hung like a clock pendulum, swinging back and forth in midair. Below he saw only cold and dark. On either side gleamed blue-white ice impossible to grip. He sheathed his sword and took out his dagger. Chipping away at the ice as hard as he could produced no results. The ice turned the steel point and prevented him from fashioning crude foot and hand holds. He resheathed his knife and looked above him. By this time he thought the others in the party should have begun hoisting him and Ehznoll up.

They hadn't.

The icy cold wind gusting up from the bottom of the deep crevasse felt like the very breath of demons.

"What's wrong up there?" he called. "Why aren't they helping us?"

"I can't see." The pilgrim closed his eyes, crossed his wrists over his chest, and began muttering invocations to the earth. Lan didn't see how that was going to help any. He held down a moment of panic. He needed a set of rungs in the ice if he wanted to get out of here. He had to help himself. He had to do it right the first time; the cold sapped his strength more and more.

If his knife hardly scratched the ice, his bare fingers would be even less effective. Using his sword was out of the question. In the narrow confines he couldn't get a proper swing. Besides, if his knife failed, there was little reason to think his sword would do better.

He shivered, wishing for a fire.

Fire.

Fire at his fingertips.

Lan Martak had never used his minor magics for anything significant before. He decided there was no time like the present to try. Holding his right hand against the cold wall of ice, he concentrated on the pyromancy spell. Flickers of spark jumped from thumb to index finger. The spell became more vibrant, living in his brain, growing, spreading to engulf his senses. Lan felt a power burst forth inside him unlike anything he'd ever before experienced.

A continuous blast of heat poured from between his fingers. The ice began melting. Lan whooped with joy and guided his miniature blowtorch inward, melting out a foothold, a handhold, another foothold. Able to stand in the melted indentations, he worked higher, the flames cutting into the ice at the top limits of his reach.

What seemed hours later, he began climbing. The pressure around his waist and upper arms from hanging by the rope vanished, and relief came so swiftly he cried out in pain. Blood returned to long-forgotten arteries. Clumsy, he almost slipped. He tried to again perform the pyromancy spell, but the toll on his body was too great. Exhausted in mind and body, he could only cling to the ice walls.

"What's happening?" demanded Ehznoll. The man turned and looked down. "Oh. I thought you'd fallen. Your weight seemed to vanish from the rope."

"What progress on top? Why aren't they helping us?"

"I don't even hear them, but the tension remains on the rope."

"Can you climb up now that my weight's off you?"

"I . . . I'll try, the good earth willing."

"Do it!"

Ehznoll kicked toes into the ice and crusted snow, found footing, and began to creep upward. Lan helped as much as he could by continuing to melt handholds for himself and keeping the weight of his body off Ehznoll's waist and back, but the more he worked, the tireder he became. All too soon, the fire at his fingertips flickered out and refused to return.

"I'm almost at the top. But there's nothing to hang on to!"

"Call out. Get someone to give you a hand."

"Th-there's no one up here."

"Damn," Lan muttered under his breath. Cold white plumes gusted out and fogged the air between his face and the ice wall he clung to so precariously. He felt alone in this frozen world, abandoned. And from the sound of Ehznoll's voice, he did, too. His beloved earth god had betrayed him.

"A rock!" Triumph rang in Ehznoll's voice. "I've got a rock. The good earth rescues me!"

"Hurry. I can't hold on much longer." Lan Martak's fingers and toes tingled with frostbite, even after their daring flirtation with fire. His back ached from the unnatural, cramped position, and the constant fear of falling even deeper into the bowels of the miniglacier gnawed at his courage.

A sudden yank pulled him off his carefully formed handholds. He cried out in fear, then felt the rope around him jerk again. Higher and higher he moved, every tug bringing him a few inches closer to the elusive slit above. Iron-grey sky appeared, then white snow banks, then the lofty crag of Mount Tartanius itself. He fell forward, panting, his fingers clawing at the frozen plain. Never had ice felt better.

"Where are the others?" he demanded.

Sitting up, he saw that Abasi-Abi had cut the rope just behind Ehznoll when the pair had fallen into the crevasse. Some magical holding spell had pinioned the rope to the ground. This was all the mage had done. He and the others had then left.

"I'll kill him, I swear I'll kill him!" Lan's hand went to his sword, but reaction made him shake too much to even make the dramatic gesture of drawing and brandishing it.

"Why?" asked Ehznoll. "We are safe."

"He left us to die."

"We didn't. The good earth saw our need and rescued us."

"If you hadn't reached that rock, we'd have frozen in the crevice. There isn't anything else around strong enough to hold your weight."

"The good earth provided."

"Abasi-Abi should have saved us. That's why we were tied together."

"Friend Lan Martak," came Krek's greeting. He turned and saw the giant spider trotting across the ice field. The eight legs and wide stance provided enough traction and safety that the arachnid had no problem stepping over the occasional crevasses he encountered. "You are safe. I ranged ahead, scouting your path. Abasi-Abi caught up and told of your plight. I came as quickly as I could, though I see now the effort was wasted. You are safe."

"I'll kill him," said Lan. "He left us."

"Do not blame him, friend Lan Martak." The spider edged around, large dish-sized brown eyes staring at Ehznoll. "He encountered a small band of grey-clad soldiers. They engaged him."

"And?"

"And he caused them to . . . vanish."

"Did you see any of this?"

"No, but he told me about when he caught up with me on the upper slopes. I inquired. He said there was no woman among their number. I do not believe it is the same party we left cocooned in the foothills."

Lan sat in the snow, wondering if the sorcerer

had lied to Krek. The spider could be very innocent when it came to human duplicity, yet the story
had a ring of truth to it. They hadn't been harassed
by the grey-clads since the foothills. It seemed
unlikely that the band led by Kiska k'Adesina was
the only one—and time enough had passed for her
and the other three to get free of Krek's silken
bindings—if not to follow, then to warn other
squads.

"If he defeated them, why didn't he help us
afterward?" demanded Lan.

The spider shrugged, shaking all over.

"The man is disagreeable," said Ehznoll. "I find
it difficult to believe he is a true believer in the
earth."

"How far upslope is he?"

"Less," Krek said, "than an hour's walk."

"Yours or mine?"

"Mine."

"That makes Abasi-Abi more than three hours
away. Let's camp here for the night, then catch up
with him as quickly as we can tomorrow. Krek,
will you stay with us? I don't want to split forces
again."

"There is little else to amuse me," the giant
spider declared, squatting down and pulling in long
legs.

The dying embers of the campfire cast a dull
orange pallor over Ehznoll's face. Lan studied the
man, wondering what drove him.

Ehznoll glanced up and seemed to understand.

"I'm a minor noble," he said without preamble.
"Born in Melitarsus, grew up there in the court of
the Suzerain." Lan listened more attentively now.
"The city was different, in the old days. Look, do
you know what this signifies?" Ehznoll reached
under his robe and pulled forth a battered, dirty

grey scarf. For a long moment, Lan studied it, wondering why he should know.

It came to him in a rush.

"The flyers wear white scarves. You were one of the air glider corps?"

"That I was," confirmed the pilgrim, sadly shaking his head. "I sinned constantly. I forsook the sweet earth for the sky. The freedom I felt was illusory. To soar, to catch the thermals and rival the sun itself, those were my sins."

"The glider pilots do necessary work for Melitarsus. While I was there, they scouted for grasshopper incursions into the city."

"They do that still? Good," he said, "because it is their only worthwhile function. On the ground, the nobles treat the pilots with respect, with awe, with more. The glider corps is always invited to Nashira's parties."

Ehznoll stared into the fire, his eyes no longer fanatical. He was a man remembering. Not all the memories were fond ones.

"I discovered the endless orgies weren't for me. The more I extended myself trying to tell the others of the errors of their ways, the more they laughed at me. Flying became more than a job for me; it became an obsession. Only in the air could I be free of Nashira and the witch spells she uses."

"What spells?" asked Lan, trying to sound casual.

"Compulsions. She is a wizard." He laughed at his slight pun. "She is extraordinarily adept at making others do as she bids. Nothing overt. Nashira is always subtle."

Lan had learned that the hard way.

"And her unholy tastes," said Ezhnoll, the light of a fanatic returning slowly to his eyes. "Her son! Kyle is a monster! He . . . he does things so unspeakable even I, a holy man, dare not dwell on the description lest I be subverted."

"Is a child so evil?"

"Worse. Nashira is subtle. Kyle's raw wizardry shakes the foundations of Melitarsus itself. One day, when he deposes his mother, then will be carnage."

"What of the grey soldiers? Why doesn't Nashira fear them?"

"She sees no threat at all to her power. She is a supreme egotist. Nothing that will disturb her can be uttered within her hearing; that is her greatest spell and that will be her downfall. Pleasure," growled the pilgrim, "is all she lives for.

"I found the true faith one summer. A pilgrim on her way to Mount Tartanius stopped in Melitarsus for the night. We ... we shared cultures and I found hers better. I became a disciple of the good earth."

"Just like that?"

"She was very persuasive. And the night was long."

The embers died down, only small hissings sounding when an occasional snowflake touched their still-glowing hearts. Ribbons of white smoke curled upward, to be caught and dazzled by the eddies of wind whirling around the edge of the mountain.

"I left it all behind. The court of the Suzerain, lovely Melitarsus, the soft living, everything. Even the flyers." Ezhnoll touched the ragged scarf, his fingers almost caressing its silken length.

"You miss it?"

"Never!" Emotion flared in the pilgrim's face. He crammed the scarf back into the neckline of his robe and rubbed his hands on the grimy sides as if absolving himself of some guilt. His eyes blazed more brightly than the fire ever had. Religious fervor swept through him, renewed, renewing itself, feeding on itself until it boiled forth. "I found all that lacking in Melitarsus society. Inner peace came to me."

"What of the pilgrim who converted you?" asked Lan, curious.

Ehznoll didn't hear him. The pilgrim had become lost in his own religious rapture.

"The good earth provides for all. We rise from its dusty depths, only to return. It is what we do between rising and returning that matters. We do not worship the soil enough, nourish it, nurture it. We should. We must!"

He continued on. Lan realized that Ehznoll maintained a normal appearance as long as his religion wasn't discussed. Touch that subject and he became an orator, a proselytizer, a fanatic unable to reason beyond the dogma he'd been taught. Seeing that the mysteries of Melitarsus weren't to be solved for him, Lan pulled up his cape and leaned back against the warm bulk of Krek's abdomen. He positioned the magical breathing mask so that the eyeholes were properly placed.

He stared into the dying glow of the fire—there was no more wood to be found—and felt his eyelids sinking. Sleep came.

Sleep, but not peace.

The scene blurred, turned, twisted around him. He finally recognized it. Waldron's audience chamber. Before the would-be ruler stood a man and a woman: Lyk Surepta and Kiska k'Adesina.

"A new world. Commander k'Adesina," said Waldron, "take a regiment into this world for me, make it mine—ours!"

Waldron's human figure faded, a death's head superimposed. Twin shafts of ruby light blazed forth. Lan cowered from Claybore, turned to Surepta and k'Adesina for aid against this inhuman enemy. They laughed, Kiska departing after blowing a kiss to her lover and husband. Surepta bowed to the fleshless skull, then reached out.

The dream flowed like water in a stream, rippling, changing, finally clearing.

Surepta raped Inyx.

"I'll kill you!" raged Lan Martak. He tried to stop his enemy, but legs felt leaden and arms refused to lift. Surepta laughed, taunted him, dared him to act.

Twin shafts of ruby light bathed Lan. He screamed in agony. The nightmare scene flashed by, his sword spitting Surepta but the man refusing to die. Kiska waving a mailed fist at him. Waldron pointing. And above all the combatants floated Claybore's skull, oyster-white and mocking, the eye sockets leaking their deadly red glow.

"Escape?" came Claybore's mocking tones. "You cannot escape. You will die, toad. No one opposes me, no one! You will die!"

"No, no, *no*!"

Lan awoke, drenched in a cold sweat. On either side of his body rested Krek's legs. The spider stirred, head lifting and one eye studying his friend.

"Are you dying?" he asked in concern. "You fragile humans die at the oddest times."

"I—nothing."

"You also have the oddest 'nothings' I have ever experienced."

"Just a nightmare. I . . . I dreamed of Claybore and Surepta and Kiska."

"And Inyx?"

"I couldn't help her, Krek, no matter how much I tried, I couldn't help her."

"Claybore works his magics directly in your brain. If you turn back now, he wins easily, unopposed. It is all so apparent. Good night, friend Lan Martak."

The spider's eyes closed and in seconds the creature slept again. Lan wished he could find rest that easily. He feared staying awake; he feared going back to sleep even more. The visions haunting him had been too real to bear.

He stared, unseeing, until the greyness that marked dawn turned into bright yellows and oranges. A new day started, a new day filled with inimical magic and physical danger.

CHAPTER ELEVEN

Nightmares stalked him, even during waking hours. He hallucinated hideous sun demons, melting men, giant behemoths, attacking mushroom people, an entire gamut of phantasms that threatened his life. One small slip, one instant of panic, and Lan Martak would dive over the edge of mighty Mount Tartanius.

The nightmares weren't real; the death caused by reacting to them was only too real.

"Krek, he's waging war on me and I can't fight him. He's too strong."

"Claybore's power is weak."

"What? How can you say that? He ... he's driving me out of my mind." Lan shuddered as a three-headed winged creature surged upward from behind a rock. Not even the rock was real.

"If he had true power, he would slay you outright. These visions are intended to cause you to bring injury to yourself. He battles you to the full extent of his power. If you stop him now, you have stopped his worst."

"I don't know," said Lan, but the idea appealed

to him. To combat a sorcerer so powerful and win fed his vanity.

"The Kinetic Sphere is the source of Claybore's power. When he regains it, do you think he needs to send insignificant little visions? He is now weak and attempting to frighten you. How he must fear that you will succeed where he is failing."

"Failing? Claybore?"

"Is it not obvious?" asked the spider. "We make good progress. Not as good as if I went on ahead, but good, considering that so many humans are involved. Claybore's pace must be far less swift. He works to slow us through you by giving insignificant little visions. Nothing more."

Lan slammed back against a cold rock cliff as a flight of bees swarmed past him. He closed his eyes and took a deep breath. The "insignificant little visions" were potent enough. Yet the spider was right. With the Kinetic Sphere, Claybore's options extended considerably. He wouldn't attack in dreams, ambushing from sleep, pouncing on unguarded moments. Claybore's way was one of power, direct, swift, deadly.

"I seem to be able to hold back his outright invasion of my mind," said Lan. "That may be why he's restored to the illusions."

"Your magical perceptions have improved drastically." The spider made it a statement of fact.

Lan started to protest, then considered. Krek had seen what he hadn't. In Melitarsus, he had been under the Suzerain's geas, yes, but not so strongly as the spider. He had been able to break away, the magical tendrils appearing weakly clinging; for Krek they had been steel cables. Even more to the point, Krek had been able to escape with him, as if the human's mere presence was enough to loosen the magics.

The fire spell he'd used to melt footholds in the

ice crevasse, usually only of short duration, came more easily to him than ever before: He had maintained it for several minutes, even if the effort did eventually tire him drastically.

Other signs of his growing ability struck him as obvious now. He "saw" the cenotaph as easily as Krek did. He sensed the flow of magic about him to the point where Abasi-Abi hadn't even bothered denying he was a sorcerer; he had admitted it directly to Lan.

"I *can* resist," Lan said forcefully. "My skills are improving. I might need to hone them a bit before taking on Claybore, but I *can* prevent him from fooling me with those nightmare creatures."

Even as he spoke, a man-headed python slithered forward. Lan laughed and concentrated on seeing only "reality." The python creature kept coming.

"Krek!" cried Lan in panic.

"I see nothing," came the slow words from the spider. "Claybore attacks only you. You are his worst enemy now. Fight him, Lan Martak, fight him!"

No matter how Lan concentrated, the python-man refused to vanish back into the nothingness from which he came. The best Lan did was cause the image to waver slightly, as if a wall of heated air danced between them. Lan couldn't deny the creature's existence and make it vanish, so he changed tactics. He tried to project an image of his own.

For the span of a heartbeat, a giant condor flapped above the python, talons seeking out a grip on a potential dinner. Lan shuddered and dropped to his knees, weakened by the effort. The python creature remained; his condor had vanished.

"If it's not there, it can't hurt me," he said. The python struck—through him.

"Lan Martak, what is happening? You appear pale and drawn."

"This is a battle of wits, and I'm almost out of ammunition," he told his friend. "Let's hurry and catch up with Abasi-Abi. I hope he can help me."

"I shall gather up Ehznoll. He still prays to his gods of the earth."

The tattered pilgrim knelt some distance away from the silent battlefield, praying, chanting, going through rituals that made no sense to either human or spider. Lan watched and marvelled. For Ehznoll life was simple. Pray, be answered or not, have faith. No matter that experience put the lie to what he claimed. Belief triumphed continually.

Lan Martak had to put the faith in himself and his own abilities if he wanted to survive. He closed his eyes and tried to ignore a giant spinning turtle with fire leaping from its shell.

"At last," he panted. The breathing device aided him greatly—without it Lan wouldn't have lasted ten minutes—but it didn't provide all the oxygen he needed.

"It is indeed Abasi-Abi and the others," confirmed the spider.

"Praise be!" cried Ehznoll. "Just in time to join them for vespers." The pilgrim raced forward to be with Melira and the others of his group. He had harangued all day long about converting Lan to his earth religion, then shifted in the last minutes to telling how he intended to proselytize those men with Abasi-Abi.

"I certainly agree. Praise be—that he's out of my hearing."

Lan had scant chance for quiet. Abasi-Abi stalked over and stood before him, hands on hips and face like a mountain storm.

"Where have you been?"

"That's an interesting question from someone who tried to strand Ehznoll and me at the bottom of a crevasse. You deserted us!" Lan took a step forward and felt a blow to the chest, the twin of the one Abasi-Abi had given him before. This time his rage alone nullified the burning impact. He grabbed the sorcerer by the collar and lifted until the old man's toes barely touched the ground. He shook him hard.

"Put me down!"

"I ought to throw you over the cliff!"

"Put me down!"

Lan did, but not because Abasi-Abi commanded it. Behind, he saw a giant snow leopard. The creature made no sound. Its smoothly flowing muscles brought it closer, ever closer. The tiny red eyes poured out nothing but pure hatred. It reared, pawed the air with claws fully six inches long, then padded closer.

The sorcerer turned and looked, then faced Lan.

"He's doing this. Why didn't you tell me he was doing this to you?" The mage's fury washed over Lan like an avalanche. He felt cold and buried and cut off from the world. When hot winds slashed at his face, he cowered back. Abasi-Abi's rage mounted. No longer did Lan worry about the puny visions sent by Claybore. Abasi-Abi held his full attention, presented immediate danger. Krek had been right about Claybore; that sorcerer's power was stunted.

Abasi-Abi was near, mad, powerful.

Lan fell to his knees under the flame winds charring his flesh. The snow evaporated around him, became fog, then boiled away. Squinting at the sorcerer, all the man saw was a ball of incandescent gas. He tried to call out, to beg Krek for aid; then something snapped inside his head.

Krek wasn't the one to ask for aid. The firestorm raging would ignite his furry legs and incinerate the spider in a second. Lan had to fight this battle himself.

He fought. He fought as hard as he could, with the few tools at his disposal. His own pyromancy spell was pathetic in comparison with the ones used by Abasi-Abi, yet it was all he had. Healing chants worked too slowly, and there wasn't any obvious way of using them to combat the tide of magic sweeping over him.

Lan lifted thumb and forefinger, set up the bright blue flame leaping from one to the other. Enough for starting campfires, but not enough to counter the flames devouring him. He closed his eyes and imagined the tiny flame high overhead, working against the leading edge of a snowbank, melting the underpinnings of half a mountain of snow.

A deep rumbling sound shocked Lan out of his trance. His minuscule flame died.

Both he and Abasi-Abi were caught under an avalanche of snow brought down from the side of the mountain. The wash of snow extinguished the sorcerer's spell even as it buried him. Lan turned and arched his back, trapping a small amount of air even as more snow thundered down off the mountain. When the rumblings stopped, Lan was trapped in his tiny snow prison.

"What now?" he asked himself. The air came stale and choking, even with the magical breathing aid.

As he spoke, the answer presented itself. He'd used his pyromancy to bring down the snow, he could also use it to remove the snow. With a snap of his fingers, flame jumped from finger to finger. Like a knife slicing through water, he cored out a tunnel to daylight.

The last rays of the setting sun caught him fully in the face as he emerged.

Abasi-Abi had already burned his way out of the snowbank, but the brief snow bath had cooled his ire.

"We need to speak," was all the sorcerer said.

Lan helped the others free of the snow, glad that none had been hurt as a result of his tentative magics.

"You do more than sense magic," accused the sorcerer. Abasi-Abi sat beside the small campfire across from Lan, peering at him as if he had sprouted wings and horns.

"A few minor spells, that's all."

"Minor," scoffed the mage. "Hardly. The first blast of flame should have cindered you."

"I was lucky."

"No one is lucky against me. More powerful, yes, but not lucky. From the first I sensed in you a power, a different sort of power. Inexplicably, it continues to grow. You are maturing into a mage of considerable power; such a transformation normally takes years." In a more wistful tone, he added, "With me it took even longer."

"All I can do is the single pyromancy spell and some small healing spells."

"You ward off magics too well for those to be your only power."

Lan considered this. He had been able to break free of Nashira's spell in Melitarsus, while Krek had failed. And he'd done well enough against Claybore's army of visions; they hadn't harmed him even if they did frighten him with their apparent reality.

"Still, you helped me," Lan said.

"What? When?"

"Back when we'd first met. Claybore came to me in that vision. The ruby beams from his eye sockets reached out for me and you turned them aside."

"*What!*"

The sorcerer's shriek brought the entire camp awake. Seeing nothing menacing, they slowly turned over and went back to sleep, mumbling about the unwonted disturbance.

"You must have helped. I couldn't fight off Claybore by myself."

"You know of him?"

"Of course. And you know I do. We . . . in that dreamworld, the three of us fought. Right after we'd joined forces at the base of the mountain."

"I never defended you. You did it by yourself, unconsciously perhaps, but by yourself. I'd never aid another. Too risky."

"I held off Claybore by myself." Lan actually impressed himself with the idea. He remembered all too well the decapitated sorcerer's power.

"What do you know of him? How do you come to battle him?"

"Not so loud. I'm afraid Ehznoll thinks Claybore is some sort of new god to worship. Ehznoll saw one of the visions sent and thinks it some divine revelation."

"Over the rim with Ehznoll," snapped Abasi-Abi. He leaned forward, hands on knees. "What of Claybore?"

Lan quickly outlined his battles with the decapitated sorcerer, his vow to stop him and his grey-clad soldiers, and ended with his dedication to joining again with Inyx.

"I feel responsible for her plight," he explained. "Many times, she could have gone on her way and been safe. She chose to fight alongside me; I owe her for that, if nothing else. She's lost between worlds, and it's my fault."

"You know that, too," said Abasi-Abi, rubbing his temples. "You know much for someone who professes to know so little. Your skills are being brought out with every new contact with Claybore. His attacks are a catalyst for your power. Never have I heard of such a thing, but such natural talent must exist. You are it."

"So you see why *I* want to stop Claybore. What's your interest in him?"

The old sorcerer leaned back, arms crossing over his thin chest. A sly look came to his eye.

"The same as you. To keep him from spreading to all worlds along the Cenotaph Road."

"There's more," accused Lan. "And I don't need magic to tell me that."

"Very well. I shall tell you, for what good it'll do you. Our battles date back a long, long time. Claybore and I are ancient enemies, from two continually warring worlds along the Road. I won't pretend that my motives are as altruistic as yours in this matter. He has wronged me many times, and I him. But when I discovered he spread his influence along the Road, I knew I had to stop him."

"Why?"

"There are many magical artifacts along the Cenotaph Road. Claybore was denied them once, by a mage vastly more powerful than either he or I combined. He would regain them."

"You want them for yourself, is that it?"

Lan wondered what the Kinetic Sphere meant to Abasi-Abi. It certainly proved potent in untrained hands; what might it do with proper magical training?

The harsh laugh greeting him surprised Lan.

"Hardly. I want to destroy them, if I can. Only Claybore can use the artifacts. I would deny them to him permanently. This will prove a feat beyond even the original divestiture."

"Why is that?"

"You wouldn't understand."

Lan felt irrational anger at this. He was being treated like a small child told he wouldn't understand—until he grew up. He deserved better. After all, hadn't he successfully withstood Claybore's most vicious attacks?

"Try and make me understand."

"Very well. A magical relic once belonging to Claybore rests atop this mountain."

"I know," said Lan. "When we were in the world between worlds, I almost got it away from him."

"You failed? You had the chance and you failed?"

Lan felt the rising forces of magic around him, radiating outward like ripples from a rock tossed into a still pond.

"Calm down," he said. "I failed once. I won't fail again."

"Claybore makes better progress to the summit than we do. He will arrive long before we can," Abasi-Abi said angrily. "And this race is unnecessary. If you'd only stopped him when you had the chance!"

"I'm not so sure we aren't ahead of him," contradicted Lan. "And arguing about my failure between worlds won't change the past."

"It can."

"Not now," said Lan, wondering if the sorcerer meant what he'd said in a literal sense. To change history . . .

He shrugged it off. He had to sleep. The day had worn him down, and the magics had left him as weary in mind as the clinb had in body. He made a quick circuit about the encampment, saw that Ehznoll and his pilgrims had snuggled down under their pathetic tents to keep the evil sky from stealing their souls, then curled up near a fire and drifted off to sleep.

No illusory nightmares disturbed his sleep.

Lan Martak tossed and turned, then half-woke. He rubbed sleep from his eyes with an icy hand

and wondered what troubled him. Claybore's nightmares were strangely absent. He sat up and glanced around. Nothing. He lay back and soon drifted again to sleep, the uneasiness gnawing at the fringes of his consciousness like a cat worrying a mouse.

The moaning of rock moving sounded over the faint wail of the wind. Huge dark shapes moved with barely perceptible progress toward the camp. Heat radiated from each sleeping human, heat attracting the creatures. They rolled closer, ponderous and stony. Tiny rocks circled one tent holding a pilgrim. The stones crowded closer. The man inside cursed as a flailing elbow smashed into rock.

Larger stones rolled up. A boulder joined them. The man's curses were replaced by a high-pitched scream as the rocks, in a concerted effort, all rolled over him, crushing life from his struggling body.

His death screams were caught on the wind and smothered. Even those sleeping a few feet away didn't hear.

The smaller stones ground themselves down into the bloody pulp remaining, while the larger rocks moved on—to another victim.

And another and another and still another.

The sentient rocks circled Lan Martak, waiting for their larger companions to come.

The human slept on, dream-free but restless.

CHAPTER TWELVE

No nightmares. Sleep, calm, restful sleep. Nothing more. Lan Martak awakened again, uneasy. The sensation of imminent doom hung over him and made the man sit up. When Claybore attacked through the dreams, he had something to fight. Now only a nebulous feeling of danger nudged at his mind.

That made him more anxious than outright attack.

He peered out and saw nothing but rocks and the cold, black, fire-lit sky. The stars overhead had multiplied in crazy profusion until the gleaming blanket covered a thick belt from horizon to horizon. Rather than hide from such beauty, as Ehznoll and his followers did, Lan Martak revelled in it. He took a deep breath, sucked in thin, frigid air. The shock to his lungs brought him completely awake. He sighed at the feeling returning to his body. He needed rest after his battles, and here he unconsciously did all he could to awaken his slumbering muscles.

He took another deep breath, this time scenting the miasma of life. He frowned. Life at this elevation, both animal and vegetable, proved sparse. The scent of animals came even more strongly when he turned and faced the outer rim of the broad ledge on which he and the others had pitched camp.

"Who's there?" he said softly, seeing a small movement. The shadows hid further movement, but his ears caught the scrape of rock on rock.

Before he could say another word, rocks pelted his face and arms. Startled, he fell back—and felt the boulder convulse. His shock at this unexpected yielding saved his life. Lan flinched, as if burned by torches. The rock rolled forward, crushing his blanket. His jerky motion allowed him to spin onto his feet. More pebbles streaked for his face and hands.

"Awake!" he shouted. "Everyone awake. We're being attacked."

The boulder rolling ponderously toward him

blocked his view of the other humans. Lan's mind refused to believe what he saw; someone must be behind the rock, pushing it, using it as a shield. Instinct made him lash out with his knife—at the rock.

The knife scraped against flint and shot lances of spark into the night. That was expected. What took Lan by complete surprise was the shriek of inhuman agony from the stone. It cringed back as a small line left by his knife oozed thick juices.

"The rocks are alive. Use your swords!"

His own sword lay on the other side of the boulder confronting him. He lunged, his knife point digging squarely into the rock. He felt strong initial resistance, then nothing. The dagger was buried hilt-deep and produced another strident cry.

Rocks battered his legs and torso now. He saw a pebble actually launch itself directly at his head. He dodged, but not far enough. The glancing blow stunned him. He fell to his knees, slashing blindly with his knife. The smaller rocks moved faster, but the large ones had the bulk to crush him. He succeeded in severely wounding another of the large stones.

"Friend Lan Martak, what are these absurd beasts? They seem to be rocks."

"They're alive, whatever they are. And they bleed when cut. Fight them, Krek, fight them!"

"Fight?" the spider quavered. "I have no desire to harm any living beast. I feel so guilty about being forced to do so in Melitarsus. I have spoken to Ezhnoll about doing penance. He—"

"We'll all die if you don't help, Krek," the man shouted. He slashed, kicked, and shoved, finding little pleasure in almost braking his toe against immobile rock. He dodged around the slower-moving boulder, found his sword, and began slashing.

The large rocks retreated; the smaller ones shot through the air like rocket-driven projectiles. Lan spun and, more through luck than skill, split one in half on the edge of his sword. Pulpy innards splashed over his hand and arm. The odor arising made him gag. The pungency of rotten eggs mixed with the acid tang of spoiled fruit to give the dying creatures added protection; no skunk emitted a worse smell.

"How many are still alive?" he shouted.

"Us or them?" came Abasi-Abi's question.

"Us. There's no telling how many of them are attacking."

"Melira and three others are dead," called Ehznoll. "They rejoin the good earth. May the sweet dirt accept them and nurture them, as they accept and nurture it."

"Damn," Lan said fervently. He felt an obligation toward Melira. He'd saved her life, and now she had been killed. Anger fed his sword strokes. He chopped the top five inches off the nearest boulder. It screeched in agony and rolled away, leaving bloody marks every time the injured portion touched real rock.

"Lan Martak, watch out!" Krek's warning almost came too late. Larger rocks circled Lan again, singling him out as the humans' leader. He looked up and saw a pair of especially large rocks coming together in a powerful nutcracker move. He had no way of avoiding them; his back was to a sheer rock face. In front of him was a miles-long drop off the side of Mount Tartanius.

Krek rescued him with a combination of agility and strength. The spider hopped over one of the boulders, to join Lan in between. Six legs grabbed, caught, dug in, and twisted to deflect the course of the rock on Lan's right. Krek grunted and heaved. The rock spun out, over the rim, hung for a moment as if disobeying the law of gravity, then began a slow tumble downward.

Lan's hard thrust rammed his sword halfway through the other rock. It screeched its unearthly sound of stark pain, shrank back, then rolled off into the night, mewling as it went.

"That'll show 'em!" crowed Lan. The animated rocks, even down to the smallest of stones, retreated. They attacked in the dark, with geologic slowness. Confronted with faster-moving adversaries, they stood no chance.

"Yes, that shows them," came Krek's tormented voice.

"What happened? Your leg. It's crushed!"

The spider hobbled on seven legs, one dangling at odd angles from abdomen to clawtip.

"They'll not be back. I've seen to that," said Abasi-Abi, an anger about him going further than the deaths of the others. Lan thought the sorcerer railed as much against their slackened chances of reaching the summit as anything else. Abasi-Abi was as much a fanatic on this as Ehznoll.

"Can you help me with Krek?" asked Lan. "He's badly injured."

"I have no time for that. I must see if Claybore sent those rock creatures. I've never before encountered anything like them. If it is his magic that animated them, he's regained his power."

"But Krek's leg—"

"He has seven others. Let him use those."

The sorcerer dropped to the ground, head in hands. Small snippets of his chant reached Lan and made him even madder. While he saw the need to protect themselves from Claybore, the danger had passed. It was time to tend their injured— the majority of their party had already died under the crushing advance of the rock-beings.

"I know only a few spells, Krek, and I don't know if they'll work at all on you."

"Do try," said the spider in a level, offhand voice. "The pain is extreme."

"I wish Inyx were here. Her healing expertise is much greater than mine."

"She can only bandage. You must repair. I feel the insides of that leg so intimately now. Strange," the spider said in an unnaturally calm way, "I do have seven others, but this one seems more precious to me. It is as if I would trade the other seven, whole, for this single one being repaired. Quite ridiculous, since I can hardly be expected to swing well on the web with only one leg." The spider babbled on, shock obvious in his monotones. For that, Lan had little in the way of aid. For the rest, he'd have to see. Lan took the damaged leg and examined it. He felt his gorge rising.

The leg had been almost totally crushed, held to the spider's abdomen only by the outer layers of skin.

"Abasi-Abi!" he called. "I can't do anything for him. You're going to have to help me."

"Away!" snapped the mage. "I cannot find Claybore. The devil is hiding from me. I seek him . . ." The man's voice trailed off, indicating no chance of ever getting help from him. Lan Martak looked around, desperate.

The handful of survivors gave as little hope. Ehznoll prayed for his lost companions. Two others who had been with Abasi-Abi collected the gear of the deceased. One other, clutching a broken arm to his chest, completed the roster of survivors.

"My earliest days were unhappy, also," said Krek, his voice shocking Lan more and more. The eerie, monotonous tone spoke of extreme mental trauma. "I was kidnapped while still in my egg and sold to an old king. A nice man, but doddering. I aided him in brief excursions against his enemy, who later became his son-in-law. You humans perform the oddest rituals prior to mating."

"Right, Krek, don't we?"

Lan fought his own panic down as he ran fingers through the bloodied fur on the leg. He imagined a large, tranquil lake, floating above it, drifting like a feather, sinking, sinking slowly into the blood-warmth of the water, soothing, calming, becoming at peace and floating . . . floating . . . floating.

His mind ordered, Lan Martak began the only healing spells he knew.

The healing he attempted exceeded any he'd ever tried before. Minor cuts and abrasions, even simple fractures, were within his powers. To restore an entire limb—that required spells more potent than any he knew.

But he found that, once started, the process went slowly, smoothly. His panic had gone entirely. Only cool confidence remained. The elementary spells worked, but not to his complete satisfaction. While allowing one to work its healing, he began another and yet a third. He juggled the three spells at the same time, in ways he only dimly understood.

"My fur tingles, friend Lan Martak."

He couldn't answer. His mind focused totally on the healing process. Internal. Veins. Arteries. Nerves. He worked in ways unknown and unknowable. External. The fur. Talon. Joints. All rolled together in his mind as one complex painting, with himself cast as the artist. When he knew he couldn't go on for another second, he did. He had to if he wanted to save Krek's leg.

Power drained more rapidly from his body. Lan had been tired before. Now he approached exhaustion. The more carefully he worked, plying the healings along Krek's leg, the more energy he used.

Hands shaking, eyes blurring, he refused to stop. The process neared a finish—too near to stop.

"Just a bit more. Oh, just a bit more . . ."

"My leg comes alive. It hurts, but it is a good hurt. You have done it, friend Lan Martak!"

The enthusiasm and thanks gushing from the spider's mouth brought Lan out of his trance. Sweat poured from him, drenching his clothes under the cloak. A chill wind blew across the ledge their camp had been on and froze him to the bone. But inside, as tired as he was, he rejoiced.

"It worked," he said in a hushed, unbelieving voice. "I did it!"

"I never doubted you would."

Lan staggered and fell, the spider's bulk supporting him. A long leg flexed slowly, painfully in front of him.

"I do not think it will be functional for a week, but it seems intact, otherwise."

Abasi-Abi let out a shriek of pure anger, lifted his face to the cold night sky, and shrieked once again.

"You bastard!" he raged. "You inutterable, blundering fool!"

"Claybore?" asked Lan.

"You!"

"What? What'd I do?"

"Your spells. They confused my scrying and allowed Claybore to elude me. I . . . I almost had him! And that spell blanketed me."

"How could it?" I only used simple healing spells."

"Simple? You wove three of them. That's *not* simple. You fool!"

"It's not?"

"You decry your abilities, yet you fend off Claybore, you employ complex mixings of magic, you cloud the very firmament with your spells. Damn you. I almost *had* him!"

"It seems your skills grow," said Krek.

"But . . . I didn't use any spell I didn't already know."

"From what Abasi-Abi says, the mingling of those three not only proved potent in healing my precious leg, it also produced potent cloudings to his spells."

"But he's a full-blown mage. He and Claybore operate on levels I don't even know exist. How can I foul anything Abasi-Abi does?"

"He thinks you did. I must say, though, that sensation is returning to my leg in peculiar ways. Are you sure you had full control of your spell? I feel a quaking up and down that leg."

"What?"

"In fact," the arachnid went on," I feel it in all my legs. I hardly believe riders approach. We are too high for earthquakes. This feel is materially different from an avalanche. If I did not know better, I might surmise the entire mountain was coming apart."

"The ledge," Lan shouted, even as Krek continued his itemizing. "It's breaking off. Get inward of the mountain. Get off the ledge!"

He acted even as he spoke. He shoved Ehznoll ahead of him toward the sheer face of the mountain. The vibration under his boots told the story. They wouldn't make it. The ledge shuddered and sank, even as he herded the pilgrim ahead of him.

"The good earth will not allow us to perish," the man was saying in his solemn, pontifical manner.

"We're over the edge if we don't hang on," cried Lan. The world disappeared from under his feet. Frantic fingers clawed at solid rock, seeking purchase, finding nothing. He slipped, his body tumbling over the precipice.

He jerked to a halt and slammed hard against the rock face when Ehznoll caught hold of his cloak. Lan dangled, half-choked. He weakly kicked out and found a foothold for himself. He managed to pulled himself in to the solid rock, fingers and toes momentarily secure.

"Th-thanks," he gasped out. "We're even now."

"Only the earth keeps score. Humans obey the whims of fate."

"Thanks anyway." But Lan found himself in a predicament. Ehznoll clung above him and had some small chance of working his way parallel to the rock face and reaching a cut in the mountain leading inward and away from the broken ledge. For Lan to reach the spot Ehznoll occupied would require wings. He felt his strength ebbing and flowing; healing Krek had been costly to him. He now lacked strength to do more than cling.

"Krek, where are you?"

No answer.

He hoped the spider had managed to hop away on his seven good legs and find a secure spot from which to launch a rescue. The thought of Krek vanishing over the side of the mountain, to land on the hard ground a mile below, robbed him of both will and more strength.

"Ehznoll, do you see anyone else?"

"I . . . no. I can climb up and reach a chimney. Shall I leave you?"

"Do it! And get help. Krek, Abasi-Abi, somebody. I don't know how much longer I can hold on."

He averted his face as Ehznoll began a painstaking traverse on the face. Rocks pelted him; at least these weren't living and malicious. When the rain stopped, he chanced a look. Ehznoll had gone. Lan Martak had never felt more alone in his life.

He clung with fierce tenacity to the rock, refusing to look below at the impossible miles of openness between him and the ground, yet some perverse impulse forced his head around and his eyes to open. The vertigo assailing him almost caused him to lose his hold and go cartwheeling off into nothingness.

"No," he said, tightly closing his eyes, feeling the sweat pour down his face and being unable to spare a hand to wipe it away. "I won't look again."

He did.

A dozen feet below him dangled Abasi-Abi. The mage had fallen with the ledge; unlike the tons of rock, the sorcerer hadn't continued on. He hung by an arm wedged between two upjuts of sharp rock. A few inches in either direction and he wouldn't have been caught—he'd have been impaled.

His head lolled to one side and blood trickled from cuts on his face. Lan wondered if the mage were even alive, then saw the sporadic rise and fall of his chest. Abasi-Abi lived, but not for long if he remained where he was.

"I can't," Lan said. He had barely enough strength to hold on himself. ressing bare forehead against cold, rough rock, he tried to order his thoughts. Yet he knew he had to try. He had to, in spite of Abasi-Abi's curt manner and abrasive comments.

Lan Martak found an inner reserve of power he hadn't known he possessed. One small step at a time took him lower and lower on the rock face. He passed a spot sheared off by the falling ledge. The primal energy released in that rock fall astounded him; in a way, it spurred him on. He lived, breathed, thought, dared. He transcended the rock in its mindless power; he directed his waning resources.

"A little more, just a little more," he said to himself. He dropped down to a spot level with the sorcerer. "Wake up, Abasi-Abi. Damn you, I need help. Help me by helping yourself."

The mage's head rocked slightly, then rose. Blood obscured most of the man's face. One eye had been matted shut, leaving the other to peer out of the ghastly mask with insane animation.

"I can help," the mage said. "Free me, and I can help."

Lan looked at the twin spires of rock thrusting upward, at the sorcerer's arm wedged between them. With a single bold step, he twisted and changed positions. One leg remained firm against the mountain. The other found a foothold on the nearest rocky spire. Leaning forward at the waist, Lan grabbed the mage's sleeve. The heavy cloth ripped under his tugging.

"It's going to hurt when I pull you free. I might hurt you even worse after you're free."

"Stop prattling. Do it!" The old man's querulous words were also reassuring. He knew what lay ahead and didn't flinch from it. Neither did Lan.

The sorcerer screamed in abject pain as Lan jerked hard, pulling the arm free. Gobbets of flesh remained behind on the rough stone, but Abasi-Abi had been freed. Lan took as much of the dead weight on his legs and hips as possible. He swung from the waist and tossed the mage against the face of Mount Tartanius. Weak fingers scrabbled for a hold on the rock. One arm hung useless. But the old man tried and succeeded.

His first words were about what Lan expected.

"You caused this, you, you insufferable meddler!"

"How'd I cause the ledge to fall off?"

"Those spells. You kept me away from Claybore. He cast a single spell and caused the ledge to fall, and you clouded everything so much I couldn't stop him."

"You're putting a lot onto Claybore. You admitted his powers were weak. How could he chisel off all that rock?"

"It was already weakened. It's not a difficult

spell, just an obvious one—if you hadn't given him cover to hide behind."

"Let's worry about all that later, when we're safe. In case you hadn't noticed, we're still thirty feet away from safety." Lan pointed upward across the rock. As exhausted as he felt, it might as well have been thirty million miles.

"Claybore! He tries again!"

Lan Martak felt rumblings deep within Mount Tartanius. As the quaking increased, he was treated to a shower of rock from above. Even worse, the tiny ledges he clung to for dear life began to break. He'd rescued Abasi-Abi; the respite seemed temporary.

Both of them now were threatened with death. The rock under Lan's left foot broke free. He clung desperately, waiting for the other foothold to crack, too.

CHAPTER THIRTEEN

Both of his feet dangled above infinity. Lan Martak refused to look down. If he did, he knew vertigo would seize him and spin his head beyond recovery. He looked up, at his hands, at the fingers slowly slipping away from the hard face of the cliff. He concentrated on the fire-making spell. It had worked against the walls of the ice crevasse; it might work here.

It didn't.

The man's concentration faded as pain washed through his body. His fingers began to jerk and twitch with muscle spasms reaching all the way into his forearms. His elbows felt as if someone had taken hammers to them. Worst of all, his breathing mask had been pulled away. He gasped for air and found none. The exalted, stately elevation of Mount Tartanius now robbed him of his life by slow measures.

Claybore would win. He'd never again see Inyx, never rescue her from the whiteness between worlds. She was doomed to wander as Zarella wandered. Claybore would win, he'd spread his insidious influence across every world along the Cenotaph Road. Those thoughts jumbled and repeated constantly in his head.

Lan's fingers hardened into steel spikes as determination gave him the strength he needed to hang on.

He almost slipped when a heavy weight descended around his neck. Abasi-Abi had fallen free and now clung in desperation.

"Y-you're choking me," gasped out Lan. "I . . . I can't breathe!"

"Now you can," came the quick words. And Lan found that he could. The sorcerer had expanded whatever spell enabling him to breathe without the mask to cover Lan, also.

"Get us out of this," begged Lan. His feet swung free. No foothold could be found. "Use your magic. Do something! I can't hang on like this forever."

"There's no magic to fly."

"I've seen the flyers in Melitarsus. What do you mean there's no magic?"

"No magic I know. Damn Claybore!"

"Yes, damn him. Now help *me*!" The sorcerer said nothing, but Lan Martak felt tingles pass along his arms, spreading from his shoulders and expanding downward through his body. His once-leaden legs came alive. He kicked; his foot dug into solid rock. He kicked with the other foot. A new foothold.

Strength pouring through him, he began to climb.

He felt the sorcerer still clinging around his neck, but the burden no longer hindered him. He had the strength of ten men, a hundred. He climbed with almost arrogant ease. He experienced in that moment the freedom Krek must feel swinging in the center of his web.

And as quickly as the newfound strength had entered his body, it began to fade. Fully a score of feet remained between him and safety above on a new ledge.

"What's wrong?" he cried.

"My power, it's being interfered with. Claybore's countering my spell." Abasi-Abi's voice sounded eons older. When Lan felt the arms circling his neck begin to slip, he knew that the sorcerer had reached the limits of his endurance.

They were still more than fifteen feet from safety.

Panic seized him, only to be replaced with a coldness and a calm he'd experienced before. His mind turned over the sensations he'd felt when Abasi-Abi's spell had begun. The effects had been similar to the healing spells he knew; similar, but not identical. Working this over and over in his mind, he began itemizing the small differences, incorporating them, experimenting, altering slightly the spells he already knew until the strength again flowed through him.

He climbed briskly, no longer tired. Lan tried to expand his spell to include Abasi-Abi but felt his control slip. He decided the sorcerer was best served by reaching the ledge above as quickly as possible. When he twisted over, he heaved and Abasi-Abi gratefully collapsed onto the firmness of solid rock.

"You know that spell, also," the mage said. "And Claybore could not block you. You fight him and win. You counter his best spells. Who are you? I should have detected you sooner."

Lan Martak's entire body went numb with shock.

He felt frostbite on his nose and fingers and toes. He gasped for air that never reached his lungs. His head spun wildly, causing him to cling to the rock for support. He passed out.

The last sight he had was Abasi-Abi sitting beside him, shaking his head, looking disgusted.

". . . and I solemnly tell you he knows little magic," came Krek's voice. Lan Martak shook his head and felt as if everything inside had come loose. He groaned and tried to push himself erect. Krek said, "I believe his current condition proves my point."

"Impossible." Abasi-Abi's voice cut through Lan's mind like a razor. "He uses spells too proficiently. He lies back, waiting for the proper moment. He pretends to be an ignorant lout. No clod-buster bests Claybore as he's done."

"Will you please shut up?" Lan moaned. "I hurt. All over."

"An effect of the spells he's been using," said Abasi-Abi, a smugness to him that irritated Lan. He knew that the spider wouldn't tolerate being proved wrong, either. He let Krek answer. The effort for him was too much.

"He heals. Witness my leg." Krek wiggled his damaged leg, showing the returning mobility. "And he uses that horrid flame spell of his to make campfires. He knows nothing else." The spider paused, then added melodramatically, "Sometimes I believe that last statement of mind is the literal truth."

"He combines spells in ways only a mage can. But it matters little if his powers are a hundred times greater if we fail to reach the summit before Claybore." Abasi-Abi hunkered down and pulled his robe in around his body.

"How many of us are left?" asked Lan. He looked

around and saw Krek, the sorcerer, Ehznoll, and one other.

"Just this small band," said Krek. "The rest, alas, are gone." He rose up on all eight legs and peered over the rim downward to the earth, as if trying to figure out the paths already taken by those lost.

"The good earth has reclaimed them, one and all," said Ehznoll.

"They're dead, is what you're trying to say." Lan closed his eyes and tried to remember the spell he'd used on the face of the cliff to restore the strength to his limbs. The use of power took too much from him physically. He might be a superman for a few moments, but he'd quickly burn out his entire body if he tried to maintain that pace. He'd come perilously close to doing so already.

But how? He failed to understand what had happened. When he'd started up the mountain, his magical abilities had been minimal, yet he'd single-handedly fought off Claybore. The bending of those deadly ruby beams had been his doing, he was now sure. But how? He'd mended Krek's crushed leg. Those were spells he'd known most of his adult life, but Abasi-Abi claimed the combination to be difficult, the weaving of three at once an ability of a master sorcerer. But how? He had no formal training. And had his increasing abilities really come on the mountain—or before? Krek had been beguiled by Nashira; Lan had been able to slip her seductive spells much more easily. The only explanation lay in the brief time spent between worlds, in the white fog. He'd felt a shifting of his senses. Had it also heightened his magical skill?

Lan Martak felt no different, except for being bone-weary. But he had to admit his facility with the spells he did know had improved greatly. He didn't know whether to be thankful for that or not. He apparently held Claybore at bay; he also drew Claybore's attentions because of his enhanced skill.

"Abasi- Abi and Morto will stay here," Krek said, "while I explore upward. Friend Lan Martak, are you and Ehznoll up to examining a more inward route? This ledge provides a space much too small for you humans. I find it cozy, but from past experience, you will no doubt say it is cramped."

"It is."

"See?" the spider said haughtily. "I go. Meet back here in one hour."

Krek flashed out with his web and vanished upward. Lan swallowed hard, thinking of the long drop under the spider's legs.

He glanced over at Abasi-Abi and Morto, the only survivor of the sorcerer's original group of assistants. Morto fixed a small dinner for the mage.

"Well, Ehznoll, are you up to exploring?" he asked. "We can eat some of our rations as we climb."

"The climb is easy because the earth now aids us. We are the true believers, the ones most beloved of the good dirt." Ehznoll piously crossed wrists over his breast.

"Stuff it," said Lan in a tired voice. "I just want to be done with this."

He chewed on jerked meat, drank melted snow, and climbed. The effort proved less strenuous than Lan would have thought. Krek had left the two humans an easy path to reconnoiter. The slight upward grade soon turned into a level expanse that opened into a chasm in the side of Mount Tartanius. A small, barren valley with high, rocky walls meandered back into the mountain.

"Easy climbing," said Lan, "if the valley goes anywhere we want to go."

"The good earth provides," intoned Ehznoll.

"It provides more than dirt, I see," said Lan, pointing. "Those look like some of Krek's arachnid kinfolk. Their webs are strung all over the valley."

Feathery arrays of spider silk fluttered in the gusty winds blowing through the canyon. Spiders much smaller than Krek—but still larger than human size—darted along their aerial walkways. Lan noticed a small cluster of them dangling more than fifty feet over his head, waiting, watching, no doubt wondering at the rare human incursion into their mountain fastness.

"They're probably as intelligent as Krek," he said. "Hola! Greetings, friend spiders." Lan waved his hand to draw their attention. A thin strand of silk drifted down on the wind and lightly brushed his wrist. It clung. He wiped it off with some difficulty.

"Martak, they are not of the earth. These creatures . . . they are of the sky. They are evil. Like your unholy friend, they are evil!" Ehznoll began backing away.

"Nonsense. They're smaller than Krek, but no less intelligent. Look. They've formed a greeting party. Maybe it's their Webmaster come to welcome us."

Lan Martak stepped forward—and a dozen strands of silk dropped down on him. He stood absolutely still, wondering about the protocol of meeting their Webmaster. When new strands came floating down, he began to get mad.

"Look, I'm not going to hurt you." He tensed his muscles and broke through the silken threads. "I mean no harm. We just want a path upward to the summit."

More web-stuff fell.

"Stop it! Ehznoll, I . . ." Lan turned and saw what had happened to the pilgrim. He had been unable to break the strands cascading over him. He lay trussed up in a small cocoon, futilely struggling against his silk bonds. One strand of sticky web had closed his lips. A dozen spiders, all human-sized, worked busily around the fallen man.

"Stop that! He's not food!" cried Lan. Unbidden, the pyromancy spell came to his lips. Blue sparks erupted from his fingertips. The nearest spider ignited in a fiery ball of shrieking fury. "Wait! I didn't mean to do that," he pleaded.

More strands fell, tangling his feet. Lan fell face forward. He twisted and began working his knife from its sheath. Overhead fifty or more of the spiders worked their spinnerets. A net of silk dropped, imprisoning him. He cut, sawed, slashed. For every silk thread he severed, two more fell. In less than a minute, he lay as immobile as Ehznoll. Only good luck had prevented one of the sticky strands from closing his mouth.

The spiders chittered to themselves. He felt their hard claws prodding him, turning him over, more silk swirling about his body. He cried out as he surged aloft, head down. The spiders worked diligently for another fifteen minutes. When they'd finished, he hung upside down twenty feet over the rocky terrain.

Wind coming from the canyon blew his cocoon so that he turned slowly, treated to a full upside-down three-hundred-sixty-degree view. A dozen feet away hung Ehznoll, similarly imprisoned.

Struggle as he might, Lan Martak didn't budge the silk strands around him. He wondered when the hatchlings would come and feast.

"Krrrrrek!" he bellowed. The action caused him to bob in a sickening up-and-down motion. He turned in the wind and only occasionally saw the form of the giant spider below. "Get us ouuuuut!"

Krek ignored him. The spider trotted over to the left side of the canyon, paused a moment, then walked up the rock as if it had steps cut into it. His feet found purchase where no human's could, and he used tiny lengths of his own web to dangle in places where even he found no footing. Lan slowly turned and saw the giant spider gingerly walk out onto a web. A dozen of the smaller arachnids gathered about.

Much of what Krek said was swallowed by the wind, but Lan heard enough.

". . . no harm. They are silly-looking, but harmless."

"Food. Hatchlings need them as food."

"Your hatchlings are better served with more standard fare. Humans provide too much protein for such spindly offspring."

"Don't insult them, Krek. Don't!" Lan called. The giant spider ignored him.

"Grubs. Those are most tasty."

"We have them. We keep them." The spider in the center of the group bounced up and down, sending vibrations throughout the web.

"Do not get agitated," soothed Krek. "I have no desire to take them from you."

"Take us from them, you silly spider. Get us out of here!"

"They provide too much protein for your young. You wish strong, lithe hatchlings, not big, grossly overweight ones."

"No good for hatchlings?"

"Not in the least."

Lan Martak breathed a sigh of relief. The tone of the small spider indicated he'd come to believe Krek.

"Then we eat. Adults need protein. We eat. You join us."

"Krrrrrek!"

"These little fellows have a single-minded determination I find most stimulating after so much human company. They seem intent on devouring you, friend Lan Martak."

"Don't let them!"

"Why the concern? All life survives by one form feeding on another. From the most minute protozoan to the largest squid, this is the way of the universe."

"I don't want to be any damned spider's supper!"

"That is very unsporting of you. They did capture you fairly."

"To the Lower Places with fair. Get us down!"

Lan felt the commotion on the web rather than seeing it. He looked downward—overhead for him— and saw a rusty-furred animal skulking into the valley. The frenzy displayed by the tiny spiders was out of proportion for the meek, unannounced entrance of a single doglike creature.

"What's happening, Krek? Tell me. I can't see."

"The canine has severely agitated them. They have even left you and Ehznoll alone."

"Then get us down, dammit. Now!"

"Such impatience. I am curious about the dog. Have you lost all desire to learn from the world around you?"

"I'll learn right side up."

"You humans depend too much on orientation to the ground. A good spider knows where his web is, what crawls over it, nothing more."

"We're not spiders. Or spider food."

Krek's mandibles made a clacking noise. Lan fell ten feet before the giant spider snagged the cocoon silk and held him. A tiny hissing and Lan felt the silk rotting away. He finally broke free of the remaining strands on his own, flipped, and landed feet first on the rocky ground. Never had solid rock felt better. Ehznoll followed soon after, failing to perform the midair somersault. Lan helped him to his feet.

"The earth!" the man cried out, when the web-stuff over his face had been brushed away. "I worship the good earth. Bless you." He dropped and kissed the thin soil along the bottom of the narrow canyon.

A gout of flame lanced above Lan's head. He ducked and collided with Ehznoll, who remained on his knees, praying to the earth. A second lance of fire ignited a strand of web-stuff dangling from above.

"Fire!" shrieked Krek. "The dog spits fire."

Lan Martak saw his friend was right. The small rust-colored animal had backed up against the far rock wall. While the general shape and size of a dog, the beast had a snout more like a pig's. Twin columns of fire blasted from that snout. The threat of fire drove the small spiders crazy. Some attacked and were cremated. Others launched themselves for their aerial hideaways, only to find the fire travelling along their webs more swiftly than they.

"It smells of filth," said Ehznoll. "I prefer the scent of the earth."

"It snorts something volatile, then ignites it just in front of its nose," said Lan, fascinated by the creature.

"It is a flamer. A creature most unclean."

Lan started to say something about Ehznoll calling anyone or anything unclean, then stopped. Arguing between themselves solved nothing.

"If you are so captivated by the creature, friend Lan Martak, why not stay?"

"Sorry. Let's get out of here."

Lan, Ehznoll, and Krek backtracked toward the mouth of the canyon. At the top of a small rise, Lan looked back. A full quarter of the spiders' webs were afire. A black pall hung over the scene, and the stench from burned fur and spider and web turned his stomach.

"They're intelligent," Lan said firmly. "They need help. I'm going back."

"To die?" came Krek's soft question.

"Don't you feel *any* compassion, Krek?" he demanded. Lan pointed into the valley. "They're arachnids, just like you. Smaller, maybe, but still of your kind."

"Do you rush to save every human you see?"

"I try."

Krek let out a gusty sigh.

"That does explain many of our problems."

"They're intelligent."

"Moderately so," conceded the spider.

"We can't let them die. The flames are sweeping through the valley. Every last one of them will die."

"It's the earth's way of cleansing its cloaca," said Ehznoll.

"What?"

"The fire cleanses and purifies. The interior of the planet is afire constantly. Magma erupts to purify the unclean land. This fire is good, even if it is brought by the flamer."

"I understand Krek more than I do you, Ehznoll. He's afraid of fire. He can see what it's doing to those spiders. But you? Aren't those creatures of your earth?"

"Are they of the worm, burrowing through precious soil? No! They eat worms."

"They eat anything they can capture." Lan held back a shudder as he thought of how close he'd come to being one of those meals. "They're thinking creatures. They need help."

"Abasi-Abi awaits us on the ledge," pointed out Krek. "He and his servant Morto might press on without us."

"You found a way up, off the ledge?"

"An easy path, even for humans, after the initial climb."

Lan felt torn between rejoining Abasi-Abi and continuing up to the summit and aiding the spiders. When the flamer snorted a gout of fire directly at one of the arachnids, catching it on fire, Lan made his decision.

"I'm going back, with or without you."

He pulled his sword and rushed back down the slope. The flamer turned bloodshot eyes on him, then seemed to scowl. The spiders it understood. They were enemy. This two-legged beast was about the same size but of different texture and color. This slowness to evaluate Lan and his intentions gave the man the opportunity he needed.

He danced around one hesitant spurt of fire, then lunged. The sword tip pinked the flamer's haunch. It tried to howl in pain and spit fire at the same time. Whatever volatile it spat choked it. The flamer began kicking, clawing, snapping, trying to avoid Lan's thrusting sword. Finally realizing its tactics didn't work, the flamer raced down the valley faster than Lan could follow. By the time the man caught up, it had relit its flame.

Lan faced a wall of guttering flame. He might get lucky and penetrate the curtain of death; he probably wouldn't be able to come close enough to do anything significantly dangerous to the flamer.

He glanced overhead. They stood under a suspiciously hanging curtain of snow. Tiny cracks ran up from the bottom hoar to vanish into a softer, newer layer above. The man had seen similar blankets of snow before. He began backing away from the flamer. Emboldened by what the animal thought was fear on Lan's part, it advanced.

Lan thrust his sword into the frozen ground before him and clapped his hands. The sharp sound started an avalanche over the flamer. Lan didn't stay to see how much snow eventually thundered down; he ran for his life back up the valley until he came to the spot where spider webs swung in the gusts of air caused by the rapidly falling snow.

"There," said Lan with some satisfaction. He saluted the surviving spiders aloft, then sheathed his sword—and found his legs pinioned by new strands of silk.

He fell to one side. More strands fell on him. He ripped skin off his left arm as the sticky hunting webs clung to his flesh.

"Krek!" he bellowed.

"Oh, very well, you silly human." Krek shrieked and chittered and drove back the horde of spiders trying to again bind Lan. The giant spider excreted the chemical needed to dissolve the cords.

"Don't criticize. Just get me free."

Even as the spider did as he was told, Lan saw the desperate straits he was in. A hundred of the smaller arachnids now populated the webs aloft. They all vectored in on him.

Webs shot and missed, some landed and were severed by his sword, still others were pulled free, but the fusilade came unceasingly. Even with Krek's aid, getting back up the slope to where Ehznoll waited proved difficult.

"Friend Lan Martak, I run out of the softening fluid." The giant spider spat out another mouthful of amber fluid to dissolve the silk cords. "If you do not free yourself of more soon . . ."

Krek didn't have to spell out the alternative. Hundreds—maybe thousands—of the smaller spiders advanced on their position from the valley floor.

"Go on, Krek, you and Ehznoll. Rejoin Abasi-Abi."

"Leave you?"

"Do as I say! Now!"

"Very well. You are being very testy about this."
Krek trotted off a few feet, then turned asking,
"Are you sure you would not like company?"

Lan Martak didn't hear his friend. He prepared
to meet the onslaught of the spiders he'd tried to
aid.

CHAPTER FOURTEEN

A silken noose circled his neck, jerked him erect,
and brought him down hard to the ground. Lan
Martak couldn't even let out a strangled gasp of
horror.

"Really, friend Lan Martak, you are being too
good to those mere-spiders," said Krek with some
exasperation. He trotted back and severed the silk
band with a single slice from his mandibles. "You
are only encouraging them to continue their ways.
No human will be safe if they feel you are a
weakling."

Lan gasped in the thin air of Mount Tartanius.
Never had oxygen-poor air tasted so good to him.

"They come after us," observed Ehznoll.

"Faster. Let's get out of here a lot faster," panted
Lan. Krek and Ehznoll followed. Eventually they
outdistanced the smaller spiders, who gave up the
chase and returned to their webs for repair and to
await another likely candidate for cocooning.

They rejoined Abasi-Abi and Morto on the ledge.
The sorcerer's disposition hadn't improved, nor had
their situation, which Abasi-Abi was quick to point
out.

"We are still too far from the summit. Claybore
will arrive before us."

"I don't know how he can," said Lan. "We're making good time. It's cost us enough lives," he added gloomily.

"Claybore is not encumbered as we are with bodies that tire. Claybore is not encumbered with fools who control their magics too poorly." Abasi-Abi looked directly at Lan when saying that.

"Look, Abasi-Abi, I'm no mage. I knew a few small spells, nothing more."

"Humph."

Lan didn't feel like arguing. What had seemed like an easy path to follow even higher up the side of Mount Tartanius had turned out to be disastrous. Getting through the valley of the spiders proved too dangerous in their condition; Krek's path up the sheer side of Mount Tartanius turned out to be better—after a while. Lan only hoped the spider meant it when he said the going got easier, for humans, after the initial precipitous climb.

Abasi-Abi and Morto said nothing as they gathered their sparse belongings and prepared for the assault up the mountain. The four humans depended heavily on Krek and his web-spinning abilities in the next few hours; then came an area Lan hardly believed possible.

"It's incredible!" he exclaimed, looking out over the small valley. "There're green growing plants, small animals. This might be two miles below us and not on a mountaintop!"

"The geological and geographical details of Mount Tartanius are peculiar," said Krek. "Never have I seen a mountain so tall also fraught with tiny valleys. Perpendicular rock is more usual."

"This is the home of sorcerers," said Abasi-Abi.

"The good earth provides for us on our holy pilgrimage," Ehznoll furnished.

"I believe Abasi-Abi," said Lan. "This is almost bucolic." A tiny catch came to his throat. This small valley reminded him of one he'd found in the el-Liot Mountains back on the planet of his birth. He'd planned on settling there eventually, claiming the entire valley for himself and Zarella.

The grey-clad soldiers, Surepta—Claybore!—had shattered that dream permanently.

"The entire mountain is of sorcerous conjuring," said Morto, speaking for the first time Lan remembered. "Claybore had nothing to do with it. One greater than he forged this rocky spire and put atop it the—"

"Silence, Morto," snapped Abasi-Abi.

"Let him talk. I'm curious about how all this came about."

"Figure it out for yourself," said the sorcerer with ill-concealed disgust. "You're the one with the power."

Abasi-Abi motioned for Morto to follow. The pair went off to fix a small camp some distance away. Krek began spinning a small web for himself, leaving Lan alone with Ehznoll. The pilgrim dropped down on a partially frozen patch of dirt and began to pray.

"So that's how it is?" Lan said to himself. "Within sight of the summit and we all go our separate directions." He turned his gaze upward toward the crest of Mount Tartanius. Drifting white, puffy clouds obscured the uppermost portion of the mountain, but vagrant breaks in the cover showed a flatness that startled him. He'd expected a needle-sharp prow instead of what actually existed. But if the entire mountain had been fashioned by a master sorcerer, it explained much—and promised more surprises to come.

The weather had been perfect for their ascent. Over two miles above the surface of the land—three above sea level—the oxygen content was nil. Lan and Ehznoll once again relied on the magical breathing mask found in the shed at the base of the mountain. Abasi-Abi and Morto existed on the mage's spells, and Krek relished the thinness of the atmosphere. But most of all Lan noted the terrain. All of the mountain continually surprised him. Valleys that shouldn't have existed did. The climb up such a towering peak required considerable preparation and skill; it had been relatively easy for them. The dangers had been present, but those were minor compared to some climbs he'd been on.

He feared the worst danger of all lay ahead, atop the mountain, up on the level area.

He hunched over, head on raised knees, tired to the core of his being. Lan Martak slept.

He wandered through darkness. He snapped his fingers and uttered the pyromancy spell. Flames danced from his fingertips and brought light to the universe. He walked aimlessly at first, then some intuition took his steps in a particular direction.

"Inyx?" he whispered. The single name boomed forth, too loud, too startlingly.

"Help me, Lan. I . . . I can't get out. The whiteness is everywhere. Help me!"

He walked faster. The light from his fingertips glowed constantly now, a source of illumination for hundreds of yards. Ahead, he saw movement.

"Inyx!"

He ran forward, then stopped abruptly.

"Am I your Inyx?" came Claybore's mocking voice. "I think not."

The sorcerer's skull floated at waist level. The eye sockets remained dark, sunken.

"Why aren't you trying to kill with your eyes?" he asked.

"Like so?"

Twin beacons of ruby death lanced forth. Again,

as they had done before, the columns of light bent slightly, going around Lan Martak's body. He knew that to reach out and thrust his hand into one of those now-curving beams meant instant death.

"I don't know what spell you use to counter my death beams. One day I shall have to find out from you."

"Abasi-Abi supplies it," Lan said, hardly wanting to believe Claybore.

"Abasi-Abi, that fool? Hardly. No, Lan Martak, you are doing it. How, I don't know. And it matters little now. I have made it to the summit of Mount Tartanius. You haven't. You have failed."

"You lie!"

Laughter rang out, vanishing into the boundless dark beyond the limits of Lan's light.

"You have proved yourself a surprisingly worthy opponent. I misjudged you. At first I thought you no more than a simple-minded bumpkin from an underdeveloped world. Now I wonder. You possess deceptive magical abilities. When I least expect it, you counter my most potent spells. Who are you, Lan Martak?"

"I'm the one who wants Inyx released from the nothingness between the worlds. I'm the one who wants the Kinetic Sphere. I'm the one who wants to stop you!"

Again the laughter, this time shriller, more hysterical.

"So noble. Tell me, if I release this Inyx from her limbo, will you turn around and be content to live out your life on this fair, lush world?"

"Give up the Kinetic Sphere?"

"Yes."

"That tells me much, Claybore. You haven't won, not at all. You aren't the kind to bargain unless you stand to gain. The Sphere gives you too much power; that means you're still looking for it."

"I know where it is."

"I do, too, but I don't have it, either."

"Fool!"

The ruby beams solidified into iron, trapping Lan, forcing him to remain immobile. The skull floated closer. The jaw clacked slightly, dead bone above banging on the three teeth clinging to the bottom jaw. Lan felt irrational dread of that skull, then calmed himself. He had no idea what spell he used to keep the eye-beams at bay, but it worked. Immense flows of power surged about him; Claybore put everything into this single assault.

The disembodied sorcerer failed. As abruptly as he'd appeared, he vanished.

Lan Martak awoke screaming, the pleasant valley stretching before him, the summit of Mount Tartanius a day's climb above.

"Stairs," he said in awe. "Someone has cut a stairway into the living stone." Lan put one foot on the bottom step, as if he didn't believe it existed. Putting weight on it proved reality.

"The good earth has prepared the way for the faithful." Ehznoll stood to one side, bloodshot eyes wide in religious rapture. He had spent the entire night praying to his earth god. After the brief excursion into unreality and the confrontation with Claybore, Lan wished he had done the same.

"The steps were put here by a mage," said Morto. The man fell silent when Abasi-Abi kicked at him.

"Is it safe?" Lan asked.

"No," came the taut, crisp reply from the sorcerer. "It is very dangerous. I must go first, to explore, to counter any ward spells put along the way to deter us."

Ehznoll didn't seem to hear. He began climbing, slowly at first, then with more energy. The closer he got to the top of the mountain, the more he came alive. His pilgrimage was at an end.

"Stop, wait, don't!" cried Abasi-Abi. Ehznoll had already climbed half of the hundred steps to the summit.

"The way is safe," said Lan. "I feel no magic. Not here." From the top, however, radiated continual pulses of energy. The spells atop Mount Tartanius were potent.

"The Kinetic Sphere is there," said Krek. "I 'see' it so clearly it almost burns my eyes."

"You don't see with your eyes, not the cenotaphs," Lan pointed out.

"A figure of speech." The arachnid had begun his own way up the stairs. Lan followed. Behind came incoherent babblings from Abasi-Abi and soft, soothing words from Morto.

As he walked, Lan cast out his senses for the slightest hint of danger. Nothing. The steps were perfectly etched into the mountain, the weather clear, his personal energy at a high. The weariness of the climb had been forgotten because of the nearness of his goal. The dream battle with Claybore, while enervating, had convinced him they were still ahead of the sorcerer. They'd reach the top first. And recover the Sphere, rescue Inyx, strand Claybore, and prevent him and his grey-clad soldiers from conquering every world along the Cenotaph Road.

So simple.

Lan bounced up the last few steps and stopped to stand and stare, Ehznoll and Krek at his side. Behind, still a quarter of the way down the stairs, came old Abasi-Abi and Morto.

"Think of the forces that did this," Lan said in a soft voice.

The entire top of the mountain had been levelled off, the surface polished to a high gloss. Looking down, Lan saw his own reflection. Over an acre of mountaintop turned into a mirror—and dropped off to one side of the mirrored plane, as if an afterthought, stood a small single-roomed stone hut. Ehznoll sank to his knees, crossed wrists, and began to chant.

"I believe this is what our pilgrim seeks," said Krek.

"Hardly seems worth the effort." Even as Lan spoke, his attention became riveted to the stone hut. His eyes didn't see, but his magical sensing ability 'saw' what lay within.

The Kinetic Sphere gleamed as brightly as if it had become the sun itself.

"Stop, wait, don't go!" called Abasi-Abi, stumbling up the last few steps to join the others. "The danger. You don't know what powers you're meddling with."

"Krek, keep him here while I go exploring." Lan drew his sword and began walking. He had to place his feet carefully; not only did the surface reflect like a mirror, it proved as slippery as one.

He hadn't walked ten feet when he felt tiny tendrils working against his face, caressing his body, holding him back. He turned and immediately located the source of the magical interference. He pointed the tip of his sword directly at Abasi-Abi.

"Old man, try to stop me with your magics again and I'll toss you over the edge of the mountain."

"Don't go. Let me. You'll ruin everything."

"You've been too closed-mouthed about your business. I can only conclude you want the Kinetic Sphere for yourself."

"The Kinetic Sphere?" The sorcerer appeared genuinely surprised.

"That's the potent magical device you seek," said Lan.

"Yes, yes, it's here, but so what? I want to destroy the other. I want to prevent Claybore from regaining his power."

"If I keep him away from the Kinetic Sphere, he can't regain his power."

"No, you meddling fool, you don't understand. You're delving into matters of cosmic scope. You can't control them. You—"

"Krek, a few strands of your web, please. Yes, thanks." He watched as the spider wrapped the sorcerer firmly in a double band of thick silk. One crossed the mage's mouth and rendered him incapable of speaking. Lan Martak heaved a sigh, turned, and began his slippery way across to the hut.

Less than halfway there, a wall sprung up in front of him, a wall even more highly polished than the ground. A perfect likeness reflected back to him. At the side, barely more than tiny black dots, he made out the reflections of the others so far behind him on the plain.

Lan moved closer; the image came closer. He skirted the wall, studying its base. No seam existed between ground and wall to indicate how it had appeared so abruptly. He came to the end of the eight-foot-high barrier and peered around.

His image wrapped itself around the edge, almost as if the two-dimensional being existed and dogged his steps.

"Well, old friend, here's where I leave you."

"No."

Startled when his image replied, Lan stepped back. The reflection did likewise. Lan studied the image more carefully now. It moved when he did. A reflection, nothing more. When he tried to go around the side of the wall, the image attacked.

Quick reflexes allowed him to fend off the blow. Losing his footing on the slick surface, he slid backward and fell. The mirror-warrior stood where he had been before the attack—on his feet.

Lan retreated and regained his feet. The image diminished in size. As he retraced his path, moving closer, the image grew until it matched him in size and detail.

"Let me by," he said, feeling silly about talking to a mirror.

"No."

Coldness settled in his stomach. He swung his sword at the image and met the wall's glassy material with a ringing crash. Glass tinkled and fell to cover the plain. The mirror image had vanished. He advanced and heard Abasi-Abi crying out behind, calling him names, telling of his mismatched and illicit parentage. Lan hoped Krek would spin another strand to cover the mage's mouth.

He hadn't gone five feet when another wall appeared in front of him, also constructed of the glassy material and highly reflective. He again faced himself. Again he fought. This time his blows never even reached the wall. Shocks ran down his sword arm with the impact of the parry. Every blow he made, every parry, every riposte, was perfectly matched.

He gusted a sigh of disgust and stepped back to disengage. How could he outmaneuver his own reflections?

"Die!" came the single command.

Lan Martak found himself fighting for his life. He succeeded in preventing his own image from inflicting damage, but only barely. Lan fought, then backed away. At ten feet, the image stopped its advance, a perfect reflection, mimicking his every move. He retreated further, returning to where the others stood and watched.

"Release the web over his mouth," Lan commanded. "I want him to tell me what's going on."

Abasi-Abi sputtered when Krek pulled free the silk rope.

"How do I get by?"

"I . . . I don't know. This is the center of his power. The Kinetic Sphere feeds the defenses. Claybore isn't here, not yet, but he will be. Only he knows fully all the defenses to be found."

"You lying piece of garbage," said Lan. "You know. You've got a spell to get by those images."

"No, honestly, I don't."

"Do not desecrate this holy place, pilgrim," said Ehznoll, holding back Lan's sword arm and preventing him from running Abasi-Abi through. "The good earth will not keep us from the temple. When we are wanted, all defenses will go down. So it is written, so it is done."

"When? After sunset?"

"No. The earth rejoices in the day, abhors the night. Night is the time for the infinite sky to intrude." Lan shut out the rest of Ehznoll's maunderings. He had no desire to be converted to the earth religion. He wanted the Kinetic Sphere inside the stone hut.

Getting past his own reflection might prove difficult. After all, how could he outmaneuver himself?

"Well?"

"Nothing," answered Abasi-Abi. "I have found no spell that works."

Lan had felt the mage attempting one spell after another to eliminate the guardian reflections. The purpose of some of the spells he failed to understand, others he sensed even as they sizzled and eventually petered out. The wards placed on this mountaintop were powerful.

"I'm going to try it again. I've got an idea."

"What is this, friend Lan Martak?"

"Did a wall pop up after I went past?"

"No."

"I'm going to try to make that happen. The spell is a progressive one. The more I try, the more complex it becomes. The reflection actually initiated an attack last time. This time . . . I fight differently."

"Hurry, fool," whispered Abasi-Abi. "He comes. He is *so* near!"

Lan didn't have to ask who "he" was. Lan skated across the surface, more sure of himself this time. After falling only once, he came to the spot littered with glass shards from his prior encounter. He hurried past. The mirrored barrier sprang up in front of him. Again, he faced himself.

"Let me by."

"No."

"I mean no harm."

"No."

He tried to walk around the image. The one-to-one correspondence of movement between himself and the reflection no longer held. The image attacked. Lan found himself fighting to stay alive. And as he parried thrust after thrust, countered slash after slash, he turned.

The image turned with him. Lan smiled to himself, something not reflected. His back was now to the stone hut where the Kinetic Sphere lay. The image fought in vain now.

Lan turned and bolted for the rude door leading into the hut. Before he'd gone five feet, a new wall sprang up before him. A new warrior, identical to himself in every way, blocked his path, while the other reflection behind still charged after him.

He glanced past the image and saw a "hall of mirrors" effect. The mirror in front reflected the mirror behind in such a fashion that there appeared to be an infinite number of both mirrors and reflections. A veritable army now faced him on either side.

Lan dodged, ducked, slashed, fought. And as he moved closer to the one mirror, his image-opponents closed in on him. Their movements were not exactly identical; some independent movement was permitted by the spells. He used this to his advantage.

He swung and purposefully missed. In the same movement, Lan whirled around and engaged the reflection behind. As he fought, he brought the images closer and closer together. Both swung deadly blows at the same time; he dropped.

One image skewered the other.

Lan felt his heart leap to his throat. He'd just seen himself kill himself, the scene repeated infinitely. His brief skirmish had confused the mirror image enough. He rose and thought the path to the stone hut now clear.

The infinity of reflections supplied a new Lan Martak. A creeping sensation on the back of his neck warned him to duck. The image behind missed decapitating him by a hair's breadth.

"Stop this!" he yelled.

"*No!*" roared a chorus, each component his own voice.

He fought, his sword turning powerful blows. He struck, "killed" an image, only to have it instantly replaced. Lan soon bled from a dozen minor cuts, cuts telling him the penalty for slackening his guard for even an instant. He battled—and retreated.

He couldn't fight himself indefinitely.

Lan Martak watched the images decrease in size as he backed away from the stone hut containing t..e Kinetic Sphere and the means to rescue Inyx from her living hell. The hut was only fifty feet distant. It might as well have been a thousand miles.

CHAPTER FIFTEEN

"I'll bleed to death."

Not even this dire prediction brought Abasi-Abi from his trance. The sorcerer sat cross-legged on the mirrored plane, his eyes focused on infinity. His chest hardly moved to indicate life. Lan lifted one arm and found it totally limp. When he released it, the arm dropped heavily back into the mage's lap.

"How long's he been like this?"

"Since you left to do battle with yourself," answered Krek. "And you are not really bleeding to death, are you? This *is* just a human ploy?"

"Thought I'd shock him into responding."

"He has been shocked into his own world."

"Morto," said Lan, "you know him as well as anyone. Is he in any danger?"

"We all are. From Claybore."

"Are you an apprentice?" The vehement head shake told Lan the last thing in the world the man wanted was to be a sorcerer. He'd seen the glories—and the horrors—perpetrated by mages and wanted no part of them. But he did continue to serve Abasi-Abi. Lan asked, "Well, then, what are you to him?"

"His son."

"I didn't think sorcerers had time for such things."

"I was something of an accident, before he became so powerful. I've always been an embarrassment to him."

"You seem little more than a servant."

"He treats me that way to always let me know how unwanted I am."

"Why not leave him?"

The man's eyes showed the first spark of animation Lan had seen. Before, Morto had been little more than a whipped serving boy.

"His goal is vital. I *must* aid him. I must!"

"You want the Kinetic Sphere. I want the Kinetic Sphere. Everyone wants it."

"You babble on about the Kinetic Sphere. It's a trinket, of no importance. My father battles Claybore to prevent recovery of more potent talismans."

"More potent?" Lan studied the plain with his magic sensing and "felt" nothing. "What is it?"

"If he hasn't told you," Morto said, indicating his entranced father, "I cannot. This I will tell you, Claybore must never regain it."

"We're talking at cross-purposes, but one thing we're all agreed upon. That stone hut is our goal."

"Contains our goal," corrected Morto.

Lan turned and walked a short distance out, thinking. He had the most unlikely assortment of men imaginable for this quest. One wasn't even a man, by the strictest anatomical definition. Krek dropped in the midst of his eight legs, one still slightly stiff, and simply sat, thinking his imponderable spiderish thoughts. Abasi-Abi floated in his trance, whether doing sorcerous battle with Claybore on some plane undetectable by Lan or simply mustering his forces, Lan couldn't tell. Morto busied himself preparing food, more to keep his hands occupied than to feed anyone. He was a pathetic figure, caught between trying to please an antagonistic father and trying to live his own life and fulfill his own goals. And Ehznoll had discovered his paradise, had completed his holy pilgrimage. What he found on this peculiar mountaintop Lan didn't know, but the man prayed fervently, a vision of divinity.

Just a few yards away stood the stone building containing the Kinetic Sphere. Lan "saw" it blazing, so potent was its trapped power. With it he could free Inyx, and together they'd go exploring the endless wonders of the worlds along the Cenotaph Road.

The problem: getting into the stone hut. The solution: Lan Martak didn't know.

The sun arced up and began to drop. Throughout the day Lan hadn't come up with any clever method of getting past the mirrored guardians and into the hut. As the weakening rays began to bathe the top of Mount Tartanius in a bloody twilight, he broke the day-long silence and spoke to Krek.

"Without light there isn't any reflection."

"How profound."

"Don't be sarcastic. As soon as the sun sets, I'll try again. The images won't have enough light to form, and I can go right in."

"Do you think it will be so easy?" The arachnid shifted his bulk, favoring the stiff leg. Lan examined it, decided all had been done that could be, and turned his attention back to their goal.

"I doubt it. But it seems logical."

"That is the problem. It is too easy an answer. The mage building this shrine controlled vast energies. I doubt he overlooked protecting his creation for half of every day."

Lan had to agree, yet what else could he do? Abasi-Abi continued in his trance, and Ehznoll prayed even more vocally than before. The night was his avowed enemy; his prayers drove away the darkening sky and put him more closely in tune with his precious dirt. Even worse, to Lan's mind, was the occasional mention in those prayers of

Claybore. Ehznoll still looked on his vision as revelation; Claybore had been in the vision, therefore the decapitated sorcerer had to be a god.

Lan wondered if those prayers might actually attract Claybore. Then he pushed such nonsense from his mind. At worst, Claybore knew they'd arrived atop the mountain before him. He already knew what lay waiting here.

"The reflection might be weaker, if not entirely gone," Lan said, more to convince himself than to argue with Krek. "I'm rested now. My cuts are bandaged. Weak light, weak mirror-warrior."

"Yes."

Lan's temper rose at Krek's innocent tone, but he knew better than to answer. He had to direct his anger outward, at the spells guarding the hut. His magic sense detected no ward spells at all. The sorcerer protecting this plain had been both subtle and strong. Even if he hadn't been, the magical emanations from the world-shifting Kinetic Sphere blanketed most wards.

Lan drew his sword and strode out, appearing more confident than he felt. Behind him Ehznoll prayed, the words following him.

"Sweet earth, protect your disciples, give us the strength to return to your opened arms . . ."

The last thing Lan wanted to consider now was returning to the earth—ready for a grave.

Fifteen feet from the building popped up the first barrier. Lan reacted instantly, his sword swinging. He cracked the wall; pieces tinkled to the plain, but the image remained. Lan moved to one side. The image followed. While his theory that the reflections would be weaker had been correct, he had neglected to consider one detail.

He still fought his own image, but now the features were in shadow, blurred, vague. He fought little more than his own shadow. And that shadow carried a sword all too substantial.

The first overhead blow from the shadow image drove him to his knees. The shadow followed, steely glints showing off blade and belt. Both on their knees, Lan and his reflection fought. The image knew his every move and countered. The longer they fought, the more initiative the reflection took, feinting, slipping razor-sharp edges past his guard, even kicking out with an all-too-substantial boot to land on his shins. When he tried the same trick, his foot found only . . . air.

Lan Martak retreated. The reflection matched his best and added tricks of its own. He fought himself and lost.

Slipping on the glassy plain, now dappled with his own blood, the man reached the spot where Krek awaited.

"You were right, old spider," he said. "It didn't work."

The spider shivered, his equivalent of a shrug, and said, "I find myself with no better idea. There is naught to string a web from and swing in. Burrowing through this glassy floor is out of the question. Can you not find a proper spell and counter the reflections?"

"I'm no sorcerer, in spite of what Abasi-Abi says."

"I overheard. You've met Claybore and bested him."

"I haven't bested him. All I've done is hold him back. There's a difference. And I don't even know how I did it. Whatever spells I used, I can't remember."

"A natural talent," said Krek, his voice gusting out in a tired sigh.

"If only Abasi-Abi weren't lost in his trance."

"But he is," said Krek. "I see I shall have to give

this more thought. Much more. I am sure there is a way in. Why else build a shrine?"

"Would Ehznoll know the answer?"

"His prayers have gone unanswered. This is a case where spiderish superiority will manifest itself, I am sure."

Krek settled back down, his dish-sized dun-colored eyes softly contemplating the distant stone building. Lan didn't interrupt his friend's peculiar thought processes. At the moment he didn't care who figured out the way in, as long as they got in to recover the Kinetic Sphere. With every passing second, Lan Marak felt the increasing pressure.

Claybore came.

Bright shafts of sunlight broke the sky apart. Lan yawned and stretched, still cold and stiff from the night spent sleeping on the plain. He hadn't dreamed, of Claybore, of Inyx, of anything. That worried him. He'd hoped for a clue from Claybore as to the key for gaining entry. He knew the sorcerer neared; his path up the mountain had been slower. But the mage held himself back, probably to deny Lan the slightest of hints concerning the spells guarding the shrine.

Krek still gazed at the building, Abasi-Abi still gazed inward, Morto fixed still another meal, and Lan still felt the need for action.

"Krek, I'm going to try a spell."

"What? What spell is this?"

"I only know a few. Some healing spells and a pyromancy spell. In spite of what Claybore and Abasi-Abi say, I don't know any others."

"You can't control the others," corrected the arachnid.

"Very well. I have no conscious control. But over these, I do. I see no way of using the healing chants, so it has to be the fire-starting spell."

"How will you use it?"

"It might disperse the reflections. A bright light in front of a mirror washes out less intense images."

"I have an idea of my own."

"Good for you. I'm going to get as close as I can, up to the point where my image appears, then try the fire spell."

"I believe we can walk up without any problem."

"What?" Lan finally heard what the spider was saying.

"Just walk past the reflection."

"The years swinging in your web have finally addled your brains. You've seen what happened when I tried. No, I'm going to see if I can't overwhelm the reflection and get through. Stay here."

"Your way won't work."

"We'll see about that." Feeling challenged, Lan walked quickly across the slick glass plain. His reflection appeared at the same place it had before. He kept his sword sheathed; so did the reflection.

Lan held up his left hand, fingers spread. Tiny blue sparks jumped from fingertip to fingertip. He concentrated on the spell, building it, making it more and more potent. His mind felt as if it slipped slightly, accepting the spell, yet rejecting it at the same time. Lan glanced up once to the image; it duplicated his actions. Fat blue sparks jumped from one finger to the other.

He thought the sparks less potent, though. He returned to his own pyromancy.

His control slipped as the heat mounted and the sparks leaped forth. Heavy garlic odor filled the air as the sizzling gouts jumped further and further from his hands. Lan felt as if his brain burned along with his hand. Never had he tried to consciously control so strong a force. He settled himself and felt renewed power possess him.

He'd doubted before he was a mage of any ranking. Now he knew differently. The confrontations with Claybore, the journey through the whiteness between worlds, the continual use of his magics and the growing scope of them, all fed his confidence and strength.

"Burn!" he cried. Flames exploded from his hand and blasted thirty feet into the air.

For a moment he was so taken by the accomplishment he forgot that it had been intended only to overwhelm the reflection-warrior. Lan turned his gaze downward from the top of the fiery column to his image, expecting it to have vanished.

It hadn't.

The reflection hurled a column of its own skyward. Lan chanced a step closer. The heat from both his and the image's pyromancy almost melted him. He felt blisters popping out on his face. His lips chapped and began to char. His eyebrows and hair singed.

Again, he retreated, vanquished by a reflection. He allowed the fire to die down into guttering ruin. Dropping to hands and knees, he felt like crying, but the intense heat had dried skin and eyes to the point where nothing came.

"I failed. I failed!" he moaned over and over.

"May I try, now that you've had your fun?"

"Fun, damn you, Krek, how can you say this is fun?" Lan held up his fire-blackened hands.

"You humans engage in totally pointless ventures. *No* amount of playing with fire strikes me as worthwhile." The arachnid shuddered at the thought of fire running up and down his furry legs, then turned and walked off across the plain, his taloned claws making click-click-click sounds as he walked.

Lan got to his feet. The pain he felt was minimal; he'd get some small measure of pleasure seeing the spider fail. The arachnid simply didn't understand what he faced. When he came to his own reflection, that would be it. And Lan would laugh.

Krek continued walking forward when his image appeared. The image grew in size as Krek got closer and closer. Lan found himself holding his breath. He let out a shriek of pure joy when he saw what happened.

"You're through, Krek, you walked right on through the image!"

The spider stood at the doorway leading into the stone building.

"Of course," he said, as if he'd been certain of success from the start. Lan hesitated. Maybe the spider had been sure.

"But how? What did you do? Some spell?"

"I reasoned it through. The builder of this shrine wanted people kept out. But not all people. Why construct a shrine no one can enter? Therefore, there has to be some criterion for entry. The builder obviously does not like those bearing arms. I composed my thoughts and did not think warlike thoughts. I simply walked in."

"Let's see if it really works." Lan cast aside his sword and knife. He took a second to settle his turbulent mind and cast off intentions of fighting to gain entry. Emotions still high, he advanced.

Fear, uncertainty, panic all assailed him when his image appeared. He had done battle with himself and lost.

This time there would be no battle. He came to enter the shrine, not to fight to gain entry. His mind turned from warlike thoughts to more tranquil ones. He desired entry into the shrine. He meant no harm. His intentions were peaceful.

He walked forward. The reflection advanced until they were nose to nose. Lan calmed himself still more and took still another step—past the image.

"I made it, too!"

"Naturally," said the spider, sniffing haughtily. "I told you it would work."

Lan hurried forward, then stopped at the door. His magic sensing ability burned like a star in the night. He "felt" and "saw" the Kinetic Sphere within.

"It's here, Krek. We beat Claybore to it."

He straightened, pulled back his shoulders, and went in to reclaim the magical device that would solve all their problems.

CHAPTER SIXTEEN

He waited for lightning to strike him dead. Lan paused just inside the doorway, straining his every sense for some hint of what to expect. The odor from the inside of the stone building was at odds with those normally found. Instead of a closed, musty odor, he detected only a faint hint of pine, of things growing, of freshness and springtime and warmth. The air lightly blowing across his blistered face healed, both physically and psychically. It put him at ease, made him believe the world could be better, *was* better. The quiet of the large, dimly lit room also soothed him. He felt no surge of claustrophobia, nor of vertigo. This was a room imbued with serenity. It was as if the builder had intended this shrine to be one for relaxation, for a spot to get away from the deadly rush of the exterior world.

Lan had never felt more at peace.

He took another step into the room, this time sure of himself. The room would not lash out at him with lightning bolts. He'd passed the test out on the mirrored plain. He had proven himself worthy of being allowed to savor the tranquillity of this spot.

The simple stone walls dripped water constantly, yet the temperature remained confortable. The floor was covered with a soft, velvetlike material that made walking a joy, gave a spring to his step and a surge of energy for his legs. The only other entry-way into the building was a doorway on the left adjacent wall, a door leading to the precipice look-ing down over the edge of the mountain and two miles of emptiness.

"There," said Krek, his voice low.

The arachnid indicated the dais in the center of the room. Lan didn't need any special ability to sense magic. Setting atop the altar was a small wooden box, one foot by two by one deep. Radiat-ing outward from this box came a flood of ener-gies, the powers needed to open worlds without recourse to the cenotaphs.

Inside that box lay the Kinetic Sphere.

"Yes," said Lan, his heart feeling as if it would leap from his chest. He hurried across the room and, hands shaking, touched the lid hiding the contents of the box. Fingers stroking over rough wood, he finally lifted.

Blazing like a pink jewel, the Kinetic Sphere lay in the middle of the box. A soft grey powder sur-rounded it, cradled it, held it in a loving embrace.

"Now we can rescue Inyx." Lan reached for the Sphere.

"Powers of the earth, harken!" came the abrupt command. Lan turned and saw Ehznoll not five feet away. He'd not realized the man had followed him inside. He thought the pilgrim had remained outside, at the verge of Mount Tartanius, praying to his dirt.

"He wants the Sphere, too," said Krek.

"Is that true, Ehznoll?"

"It is the heart of the earth. Our creed is such that it must be returned to the center of the planet before all can be right again. The world festers and decays because it lacks its heart." Ehznoll began a chant, a chant that made Lan uneasy.

He'd heard those words before, the cadence, the soul-searing rhythm. Just before they'd shifted worlds, Claybore had uttered this exact chant and sent them all into the whiteness between worlds.

Lan saw pink pulsating light against the ceiling, the walls, his hand. The Kinetic Sphere had come alive. No longer crystalline in appearance, it developed arteries and veins, throbbed with life, became a living organ. Ehznoll's chant had transformed it into a large four-chambered human heart.

Repulsed and fascinated at the same time, Lan found he couldn't look away. The mitral valves opened and closed, pumping no blood, but functional just the same. Arteries twitched with pseudo-life. Veins attempted to return blood from a nonexistent body.

Coldness clutched at the man as those thoughts raced through his mind. He gripped the wooden box as awful suspicion struck him.

"Be silent, Ehznoll. Don't say another word!" he screamed. The world spun about him and the chant continued. The Kinetic Sphere's outlines altered; it quaked with anticipation. The grey dust cradling it shifted as the crystal heart vainly pumped. Lan leaned forward, his eyes screwed shut, his world crumbling again. The winds of magic blew constantly around him now. This room, once so peaceful, now assumed the aspect of deadly horror. He wanted to scream, to shout out his fear; no words came. His throat constricted with fear.

Cold sweat popped out on his forehead, stung the blisters, and dripped from lips and chin. His fingers tightened on the wood box. All he could

hear were Ehznoll's chant and machinery clanking. He opened his eyes and saw Claybore.

The sorcerer had entered the same doorway they
had. The fleshless skull rested on the body of a
mechanical like those Nashira had used as me-
nials. The parody of a human sickened Lan Martak.
His hand reached for his sword, only to find nothing. His weapons rested outside, away from this
shrine.

Claybore laughed and Lan quaked inside. The
robot creature walked with irregular stride across
the room. Krek appeared frozen. Ehznoll stayed on
his knees before the altar. Only Lan could meet
this threat. And his muscles refused to obey.

"You like my mode of transportation?" asked
Claybore. "I rather enjoyed its tirelessness, although
it doesn't travel very fast. It also has a tendency to
break down on the steeper grades. Still, not having
to feed it like I would a more human assistant had
benefits."

"The craftsmen in Melitarsus made it for you?"

"Unwillingly, but my soldiers can be very persuasive. Commander k'Adesina in particular. You've
met her, I believe. A shame she cannot be here
now; she patrols the base of the mountain. A charming woman, totally dedicated. But then, while there
are only a few troops on this world, they are all
dedicated. Yes, this artificial body has served me
well." Claybore turned, holding long, spindly metallic arms away from his body to better show off.

Lan felt the sorcerer's attention slip for an instant. His body reacted long before his mind realized he moved. He launched himself in a shallow
dive that locked his arms around Claybore's mechanical legs. The robot failed to move quickly
enough to avoid crashing forward. Lan swarmed
up it, then stopped, sick to his stomach.

The skull bounced away and landed against the far wall. He fought a headless body.

The slight hesitation was all the mechanical required to twist free. It scurried on hands and knees to the sorcerer's skull and hoisted it back into place. Lan tried to rise; again came the leaden feeling in his limbs.

"The builder of the shrine foolishly devoted his energies to peace," said Claybore. "You fight against his spells, as well as mine."

"I can at least fight," muttered Lan.

"Yes, that surprises me greatly. For a bumpkin with no formal training, you have mastered many complex and ancient spells. I have thought long on how you avoid my death gaze, and have come up with no satisfactory solution. You instinctively protect yourself. I wonder if even you know how it is done."

"You won't get the Kinetic Sphere, Claybore. We'll stop you. We will!"

"We?" mocked the sorcerer. The robot body strode around while hands reached up and repositioned the head. The bone-white skull rested at a slight angle now, giving a jaunty, inquisitive air to the being. "Who is this 'we' you refer to?"

"Look, fool. A mountain arachnid. Krek. He is immobile, held firmly by my spells. His courage is a fragile thing. A few reminders of the time spent in Nashira's arena and—"

Krek emitted a shrill chittering noise that tore at Lan's heart. The spider's chocolate eyes widened and his body convulsed, folding in upon itself until it looked as if he might totally vanish.

"See? Memories are such potent weapons. I had no idea the Suzerain of Melitarsus did those things to him. His mind, of course, conjures up far worse tortures than any outsider could produce. I simply release his imagination for . . . instruction."

Lan fought against the spell holding him pinned like a butterfly. He made slow progress back toward the wooden box on the altar containing the Kinetic Sphere. While he had no plan, could not expend the effort to make one, he realized the Sphere was the most potent weapon against—and for—Claybore.

"Krek's courage diminishes with every passing moment. If I allowed this mental fantasizing of danger to continue, he would die of fright. So, he cannot be part of this 'we' you refer to. Perhaps you mean this wretched creature. This pilgrim Ehznoll. Once a valued flyer on this world, but now a worthless parasite sucking up dirt and calling it religion."

The mechanical went to where Ehznoll still knelt and prayed, his lips working silently on new and more righteous chants. A metallic foot kicked out and sent the man sprawling. Ehznoll's wrists remained crossed over his breast and his eyes never left the altar. He had achieved his paradise, the end of a long pilgrimage, and none robbed him of his moment of rapture.

"He controls many spells you do not. You never realized this, did you, Lan Martak?" The skull turned and faced Lan. "Go on, struggle. Try to reach the altar. I enjoy watching your pitiful efforts."

Lan continued to fight. Claybore toyed with him, but the sorcerer did not kill him outright. That led Lan to believe, rightly or wrongly, that Claybore was still unable to muster sufficient strength. The spells holding Krek took a considerable amount of strength. Further energy went into immobilizing Ehznoll. And the more Lan fought, the weaker the spell holding him became. Claybore boasted of his ability, but the three of them together strained that ability to the limit.

"In fact, allow me to give you a preview of what

awaits you." The robot-creature turned so that the eye sockets of the skull pointed directly at Ehznoll. Twin beams of ruby light lashed forth, bathing the pilgrim in a wan, ruddy glow.

Ehznoll screamed in agony.

"You are not of the earth!" he shrieked. "You defile the heart of the earth. You are not the god I believed. You tricked me. You—aieee!" He clutched his sides and curled into a fetal position. Every line of his face, every contour of his body, reflected the pain inflicted by Claybore's death gaze.

Lan watched and felt compassion for Ehznoll. In that instant, Ehznoll lost much of his faith, had his tenets crumble around him. The death of a belief might be worse than physical death. Lan also felt the lessening of the immaterial bonds holding him. Claybore had gone beyond the limits of his ability when he provoked and tortured the pilgrim. He could hold, but the addition of the ruby gaze forced him to turn more attention to Ehznoll. While not entirely gone, Lan successfully fought the binding spell.

He attacked.

Again, his arms circled the mechanical's legs. This time the tackle failed. The metallic creature turned and kicked. Lan tasted blood as his lip split against the sharp knee joint. He hung on and worked his way up the body, probing, hitting, butting, keeping Claybore's robot off balance. Spindly arms crashed into his back. Legs sought to knee him in the groin. Twisting and turning in an attempt to fling him away, the mechanical succeeded only in losing its balance again. From the way it had tottered into the room, Lan guessed it had been damaged on the climb up the mountainside.

Man, machine, and skull crashed down in a pile.

Lan was as strong physically as the metallic creature; his reflexes were much faster. The man pinned his knees down firmly onto geared shoulders. He stared directly into the empty eye sockets of the skull still perched on that metal neck.

"Die, fool!"

The ruby beams leaped forth.

Pain beyond comprehension washed through Lan's body. He held on. He had thwarted the death gaze before, in the dreams, when Claybore remained at a distance. But he didn't know how he'd done it. Searing, soul-wrenching misery assailed him until he almost passed out.

The beams bent and passed harmlessly to either side of his body.

"*No!*" screamed the skull. The inside of Lan's own head felt as if it would split like a rotted melon from the force of that denial. He leaned forward, his fingers slick with sweat and shaking with fear, to pluck the skull from the mechanical shoulders.

"Stop. Don't! You don't know what you're risking."

Lan said nothing as he held Claybore's fleshless skull high, intending to hurl it against the stone wall.

"We can be allies. Share with me the rule of all the worlds along the Cenotaph Road."

"I know what you are, Claybore," he said from between clenched teeth. Lan knew if he ever relaxed, his teeth would chatter with fear. He had to strike now, while the balance of power rested with him and not the ancient sorcerer.

"Inyx! You want to rescue the woman. She dies slowly between worlds. Only I can save her."

"You lie." But Lan hesitated. He knew the deal Claybore tried to make. In return for not smashing the skull into a million fragments, the mage would rescue Inyx. Lan didn't know if he personally knew enough of the workings of the Kinetic Sphere to rescue the woman in time or not. Claybore did; Claybore could. But the treacherous sorcerer would turn on him if he weakened. No deal was sacred. Honor meant nothing to the decapitated being. If he had the chance to renege and kill both Lan Martak and Inyx, he would take it.

But what if Lan Martak didn't know enough? To strand Inyx between worlds meant more than physical death, it meant an eternity of longing for real death.

He couldn't condemn her to that, if Claybore spoke the truth about being the only one who could rescue her. The skull grew warmer to his touch. The sorcerer shifted more and more of his power against Lan, but the man tapped unconscious reserves that kept the deadly ruby columns bent away from his body, kept the spells of compulsion weak.

Lan Martak had a decision to make. Believe Claybore and rescue Inyx. This led to treachery. Claybore would undoubtedly end up with the Sphere and be free to continue his conquest of a myriad worlds. Nothing guaranteed the sorcerer wouldn't turn on both of them after plucking her from the foggy interworld whiteness, either. But to smash the skull into dust meant no help whatsoever from the mage who had contrived the Kinetic Sphere.

"Freedom, I'll give you both your freedom. And . . . and you can rule with me. There're plenty of worlds. Millions! Take all you want. I'll give them to you." The skull grew hot to the touch. The very smell of heated bone nauseated the man.

Lan decided.

Even if it meant damning Inyx to an eternity of soulness limbo, he had to stop Claybore. This might be his only chance. His arm cocked back for the pitch against the wall.

He found himself upended and dumped onto his back by the still struggling mechanical. The metallic being sat up, one long arm batting the cranium out of his grip. Lan jerked around to see Claybore's skull arch upward, then fall toward the opened box on the altar. As it vanished from sight within, a tiny puff of grey powder rose.

Demoniacal laughter reverberated around the stone chamber.

"You fool, you inutterable fool!" came a shocked exclamation from the doorway. "How could you have done that?"

Lan wrestled with the mechanical, but he recognized Abasi-Abi's voice.

"If you'd helped us . . ." he began.

Abasi-Abi waved a hand. Lan felt the robot-creature stiffen as if a knife had been rammed into its back. It melted, the metal of its skeleton turning to butter. It puddled in front of him, sizzling against the softness of the floor covering, causing a metallic stench to rise up. Lan stood there stupidly, hardly believing such a thing could happen. One moment the mechanical had been substantial. The next, it dissolved into smoking liquid.

Abasi-Abi stalked into the room. Morto stood just outside the door, his face pinched and white.

"Look, look at what you've done!" Abasi-Abi pointed. Lan gasped when he saw the dust within the wooden box on the altar restlessly shifting about, forming patterns, turning more substantial. In less than a heartbeat, the grey dust had formed a torso. The Kinetic Sphere beat like an obscene heart in the chest cavity of the armless and legless body. A thin neck reached up to join with the fleshless skull he'd accidentally tossed into the box.

Lan swore that the bony skull smiled. In victory.

"I don't understand. The Sphere—"

"The damn Kinetic Sphere means nothing, or very little. It's his *body* I've tried to keep him from," snapped Abasi-Abi. "With the body regained, Claybore's power triples. More!"

Lan recoiled when the body began thrashing about inside the box—coffin.

"Your spells are potent, Lan Martak," came Claybore's voice, "but Abasi-Abi is correct. You are a fool. Now that I've regained my body, none can stop me!"

Abasi-Abi thrust out his hands. Sheets of coruscating energy blasted forth. Lan averted his eyes, shielding his face from the heat. Squinting, he saw the ghastly skull and limbless torso sit up inside the box.

Whatever power Claybore had lacked before, he now had. Lan felt the magic flowing about him and recognized little of it. Back on his home world he'd been taught minor spells for immobilizing game, for healing, for starting fires. He'd witnessed others. Once, he'd seen a man "reduced" for a crime, turned into a sizzling blob of grease. That spell had seemed potent to him.

These sorcerers battled with magics beyond his comprehension. And he'd inadvertently given Claybore back immense power.

"The eyes!" he cried. "Claybore's eye sockets!"

The mage's deep-sunken pits began to glow a dark red. Lan thrust himself in front of Abasi-Abi just as twin beacons of death shot forth. Whatever inbred spell he used so unknowingly, it still worked. The death gaze passed harmlessly to either side, leaving Abasi-Abi and himself unscathed.

"I shall rend you into atoms, Claybore!" screamed Abasi-Abi. "Terrill scattered your parts along the Cenotaph Road to stop you. I shall destroy you!"

Ghastly laughter greeted the sorcerer's words. The Kinetic Sphere pulsated more powerfully in the chest cavity, turning from pink to a royal purple. The pseudo-heart altered visibly, its texture turning from flesh to velvet to a mistiness that confused Lan's eyes. All the while, Claybore's power mounted. Lan felt the tide of battle slowly shifting. Abasi-Abi had the initial advantage. He slowly lost it to the dismembered sorcerer.

"Remember me, Abasi-Abi," gloated Claybore. "Remember me when you reach the Lower Places of Hell!"

Lan felt as if a furnace door had been opened. Heat issued forth, driving him to his knees. He fought in ways he didn't understand. He felt tiny burnings throughout his brain, racing along his spine, turning him into one giant, raw nerve ending. Physical combat wasn't possible. He joined with Abasi-Abi to fight with magics.

And they slowly lost.

It was as if they were being forced back inch by inch. As they weakened, Claybore's power grew.

"I . . . I can't go on much longer," muttered Abasi-Abi. "I feel myself slipping, slipping away. I did not prepare adequately. I'm too old, too feeble for this. I—"

"No!" shouted Lan, shaking the sorcerer. "You're the only one with the knowledge to stop him now."

"I can't."

Mocking laughter. Lan saw the obscene skull nodding atop the armless torso. The Kinetic Sphere had vanished totally into the chest. A pearl-grey light surrounded the stone altar, light signalling the end of the battle.

Claybore had won.

"Die, mortals," said Claybore. "Die knowing I shall rule a million worlds!"

"No," came a small voice from the side. "He steals the heart of the earth. Desecration! *Noooo!*" Ehznoll rose, obviously in pain. His eyes were wide and an expression of religious fervor crossed his face. He seemed to glow more brightly than the altar. "You are a false god. You are sent by the sky to destroy the sweet earth. You cannot steal the heart. It must be returned!"

Ehznoll rushed to the altar and flung his arms around the wooden box containing Claybore's skull and torso. He lifted it and turned for the door leading to the precipice.

"Stop!" Claybore's voice carried total command. The full power of his sorcerous skill drove the order directly into Ehznoll's already numbed brain.

But life remained in Abasi-Abi. A little, enough. He sent spell after intricate, deadly spell at Claybore. Ehznoll stumbled once, then, as the pressure of battle turned back to Abasi-Abi, ran for the verge of Mount Tartanius.

Claybore couldn't fight both Abasi-Abi and Ehznoll. The sorcerer could slay one or the other, but not both simultaneously. Ehznoll never broke stride when he came to the side of the mountain. He kept running, appearing to rush out another ten feet before gravity seized him and his ghastly burden.

Abasi-Abi collapsed just as Ehznoll and Claybore vanished under the rim of the mountain. Lan shook himself and reeled to the edge. He heard a faint voice drifting up to him.

"The heart will be returned!"

Ehznoll.

He heard nothing of Claybore but saw a brilliant flash before the box had travelled half the distance to the ground. As soon as the glare died, Lan slumped. All magics vanished.

The Kinetic Sphere. Claybore's spells. Abasi-Abi's counterspells. The wards atop Mount Tartanius. Everything. He was stranded on a world without cenotaphs. And Inyx was doomed to roam forever through the white fog between worlds.

He'd failed. He'd failed in every way.

CHAPTER SEVENTEEN

Time passed, and Lan Martak didn't notice. Like a man drugged, he sat and stared over the rim of Mount Tartanius down into the mists below where so much of his life had just vanished. The Kinetic Sphere was lost to him for all time. Inyx was similarly lost. Trapped between worlds, the woman was destined to roam deserted and alone forever. And, while this was a pleasant enough world, Lan had tasted the thrill of walking the Cenotaph Road, of finding and exploring new worlds. For most of his life he'd been trapped on a single world; following the advice of an ancient being, the Resident of the Pit, he'd taken a first hesitant step along the Road. He'd lost a love, killed an enemy, and found friends beyond compare in Krek and Inyx.

And they'd used the Kinetic Sphere to explore. Now that Claybore had regained his magical gateway, nothing prevented him from marching on defenseless, unsuspecting worlds and conquering them. His grey-clad soldiers would pour forth through the gate opened by the Kinetic Sphere and bring ruin and slavery to untold cultures.

Lan Martak stared down the side of Mount Tartanius, wondering if he should follow the valiant Ehznoll's path. One step, nothing, falling, death.

A light touch startled him.

"No, friend Lan Martak," came Krek's soft words. "That is Ehznoll's way, not yours. He died for his belief, for the betrayal of his faith. You must live for yours."

"Everything's gone. There's no way off this world.

You said so yourself. Unless . . ." Hope leaped in his breast.

"No," said the arachnid, "I have discovered no other cenotaph off this world. With the Kinetic Sphere gone, the 'vision' is clearer. There are no cenotaphs on this planet opening to other worlds, though I see countless ones opening onto it. These one-way gates no doubt account for the acceptance of travellers in Melitarsus. Many have entered this world only to find ño way off."

Lan slumped again.

"Ehznoll's way may have been easier, but you're right. It's not my way." Looking up at the spider, he asked, "How's Abasi-Abi? The battle may have severely injured him."

"Worse. His son Morto tends him, as is proper."

"Maybe my healing spells can do something for him. They seem to have put your leg aright."

"It remains stiff. But then, with my weakness and cowardice, what difference does it make? I am a craven, abandoning my dear, sweet little Klawn and our hatchlings. Ah," lamented Krek, "never to see one's very own hatchlings again. A real pity, but a fate tailor-made for one as miserable as I."

Lan let the spider continue on with his self-pity. Krek had to feel as bad about losing the Kinetic Sphere as he did.

Inside the stone building, Morto knelt beside his father. The sorcerer had aged incredibly. Hair totally white, face lined as if some farmer had plowed it, transparent skin pulled across his hands as taut as a drumhead, he had come as close to death as possible without crossing the line.

"Here he is," said Morto quietly. To Lan, "He wishes to speak. But hurry. He is almost gone."

Lan cradled the old sorcerer's head.

"You battled well," he said. "I am sorry to have distracted you. And I put Claybore's head with the body. I didn't know. I thought all he wanted was the Sphere."

"You didn't know," absolved Abasi-Abi. "But for that ignorance you must now be punished." Lan tensed. "I am dying. You must carry on my fight against the evil Claybore promises. Morto will give you my grimoire. You have the native skill my son lacks in magic. You will learn all the spells you can to stop Claybore."

"He used the Kinetic Sphere to shift worlds," Lan said glumly. "I saw the flash as he opened the gateway. Do you think he'll be back to slay the rest of us?"

"No, because he thinks I am dead and you helpless. He thinks there is no way off this world."

"There's a way? Tell me!"

"First, I must tell you of Terrill." Abasi-Abi's voice barely reached Lan now. The man bent down so the dying whispers sounded directly in his ear. "He was a mighty sorcerer, the mightiest and now long dead. But he saw the evil Claybore brought. Only Terrill possessed the skill to stop Claybore— not kill him, no one can do that, but stop him."

"Is Terrill the one who dismembered Claybore and scattered the pieces along the Cenotaph Road?"

"Yes."

"Claybore cannot be killed, but he can be stopped? He needs his full body for full power?"

"Yes," whispered Abasi-Abi. "Only the skull is potent, and with the body it is even more potent, but even this combination can be defeated. The danger lies in allowing Claybore to find the arms, legs, feet, hands. Once they are joined, no mage lives on any of the worlds able to withstand Claybore's might."

"You'll live, Abasi-Abi. I'll start my healing spells. They aren't much, but—"

"No!" Bony fingers clawed at Lan's arm.

"I'll have you back on your feet again. Soon. I promise."

"Lan," said Morto in a peculiarly flat voice. "He's dead. He fought death, tried to deny it. No one can do that, even one as powerful as my father."

Lan Martak placed the lifeless body gently on the soft floor.

"He didn't tell me how to get off this world. He wanted to tell me about Terrill and Claybore, but he never said anything about leaving here."

"Here is his grimoire. He wanted you to have it." Morto passed over a small volume bound in leather and brass. Lan took it as if it would bite.

"It's yours. You're his son."

"I cannot use it. I have no talent at all for magic, much to his disgust." Emotion returned to Morto's voice and color rose in his blanched cheeks. "He was a harsh master and an unloving father." Tears choked him now. "But still I loved him and believed in what he had to do."

Together the three of them, two humans and one arachnid, buried the sorcerer. The glassy plain of Mount Tartanius's mesa proved hard to dig in, but the combined assault of Lan's sword and Krek's talons, with Morto's blind determination, finally cut the grave.

"I don't know what words to say," said Lan after they'd finished covering over the body. "I wish now that Ehznoll were here."

"My father wasn't of this world, but he is now permanently in it. May his dust and that of the world merge," said Morto.

Lan Martak looked curiously at the man.

"You're not of this planet? You've walked the Road?"

"We've followed Claybore for a dozen years, ever since he regained the Kinetic Sphere. We're from a world hundreds separated from this one."

"Did you use one of the one-way gates to arrive here?" Morto nodded assent. "But how did you plan to get away, to follow Claybore, if you failed to regain the Sphere?"

"My father opened a cenotaph on the last world we visited. The powers weren't quite right to open it in both directions. The one way-gate closed behind us. Others may follow, but we can't retrace our steps."

"Clumsy of him, if I do say so," said Krek.

"Your father knew the spells to create a cenotaph?" pressed Lan.

"Of course. Abasi-Abi was one of the greatest mages since Terrill himself. It was his misfortune to be second best to Claybore. Mages possess immense egos. It is required to perform their feats; being second best added fuel to the flames of his feeling of inferiority. Even the day's preparation while you tried to enter the stone hut failed my father. The climb up Mount Tartanius had taken too much from him physically to allow total psychic strength. He was old, older than any of us can imagine. He belonged to a different world."

"It must be in the book. Morto, is the secret of creating a cenotaph in your father's spell book? Can I open up the Cenotaph Road for us?"

A shrug, a pause, and finally, "I don't know."

Lan Martak spent the next four days studying Abasi-Abi's notebook. The details it revealed confirmed much of what he'd guessed. Waldron of the bleak world had been a mere dupe in Claybore's larger plan. No mention at all of the grey king appeared in Abasi-Abi's diaries: only an unrelenting search for Claybore, continual battle with the grey-clad soldiers loyal to Claybore, worry that the renegade sorcerer might prove too powerful to vanquish.

One spell in the grimoire sent Lan's heart racing. He composed himself, allowed the immense tides of magic flowing between worlds to suffuse his body, then cast himself outward. Like the *therra* on his home world, his spirit left his body and he roamed. Hours passed as he searched, disembodied, for Inyx. The world altered around his roving spirit, changed to a featureless plain, finally became the impenetrable white fog he'd experienced before.

"Inyx!" he called. No answer. "Inyx, I need to reach you. I need you."

"Lan?" A voice, hesitant, distant.

"Inyx! Are you all right?"

"I . . . feel . . . so . . . light. No . . . body. I . . . remain in . . . this place . . . too long."

The voice faded. Lan never caught sight of the woman but heard the fear in her words. He'd been told that to remain too long in the white fogginess robbed a mortal of body and left behind only tortured spirit. It was true, and Inyx knew it.

He had to rescue her and didn't know how.

His spirit returned to his body. The weakness hitting him made him gasp and collapse. For two days Morto and Krek tended him. The excursion had been costly for him, both in energy and morale.

"I don't see how we can do it. Not on the top of this thrice-damned mountain."

"Friend Lan Martak, there must be a way. Abasi-Abi hinted as much."

"Hints, Krek, don't mean a thing. The man was dying. He was as much a fanatic as Ehznoll. Ehznoll worshipped the earth, Abasi-Abi fought his personal devil: Claybore."

"Inyx remains in limbo."

"Dammit, I know." Spots of red flushed Lan's cheeks. He paced constantly, Abasi-Abi's spell book open in one hand. "I've gone over the contact spells again and again. They don't work for me. I don't have the experience, the control, the *knowledge*."

"While I am no mage, reading through this one indicates a path to follow." Krek's claw tapped the book, opened on the stone altar in the hut.

"That's a spell for creating a cenotaph. Yes, maybe the creation would bring Inyx out of the fog, but I can't do it."

"Why not?"

"I lack the most essential ingredient: a dead hero."

"There is one."

"Abasi-Abi won't work. We've buried him already. The grave must be freshly consecrated with those spells—and the hero's body must be irretrievably lost."

"Such as lost, meaning not recoverable?"

Sometimes the spider could be so dense Lan wanted to scream.

"Yes, lost. Like . . . oh, no. Of course."

"Like Ehznoll," they chorused.

"How could I have overlooked it, Krek? He died saving us—the world—from Claybore. When he hit the ground below, nothing but pink splotches would have been left, and those would be smeared halfway down the mountain. We can consecrate a cenotaph to Ehznoll!"

"Obvious."

Lan spent another half-hour chiding himself for not seeing the obvious, then took another hour worrying about the qualities of Ehznoll's heroism. He finally decided heroism, no matter how motivated, provided the psychic energy required for establishing the Cenotaph Road. The gateway between worlds could be opened, no matter what he'd thought of Ehznoll while he lived.

Lan Martak pored over the spells while Krek and Morto hollowed out the altar inside the hut. A special crypt had to be formed, one large enough to hold a human—or spider. But for all his bulk, Krek managed to compact himself down into large human size.

As the spider and human finished their chore, Lan said, "The preliminary spells are ready. I . . . I've improvised." He looked from Krek to Morto, to see if they approved.

"Improvised in what way?" asked Morto.

"I've sent a seeking spell into the whiteness and tried to couple it with the opening of the cenotaph. In this way, as the Cenotaph Road opens, Inyx will be pulled along and deposited on the proper world— the world onto which the cenotaph joins this one. We follow and join her."

"Which world?" the man asked.

"Which? Well, I can't say. Is there a way of telling beforehand?"

"There is. My father often cast scrying spells for days, hunting for the exact world he desired most."

"I can't do that. It . . . it wasn't in his book." Lan again felt his inadequacy as a mage. All through his preparations he'd sensed his control teetering, almost being lost. The energies he moulded were immense and immensely beyond his comprehension. Still, necessity forced him into the role of sorcerer.

"Are we going to the world Claybore shifted to?" asked Krek.

"I don't know. There's so much about this I just don't know."

"Fear naught, friend Lan Martak. You have done well, I am sure. Though, I do remember the time when you . . ." The spider's voice trailed off in memory of some gaffe on Lan's part.

"The spells. Now." Lan Martak closed his eyes

and felt the rush of power surround him. As if he stood on a beach and the ocean waves lapped around his ankles, the power mounted. Up to his knees. Control. He fought to prevent a runaway of the energies he commanded. To his waist. A *flicker*. The gateway almost opened. He sculpted the almost palpable waves around him. The Cenotaph Road beckoned. The warm, engulfing waves rose higher, ever higher. To his neck. Over his head. A moment of panic. Control. He regained control. Another *flicker*, followed by an intensely brilliant *flash*.

The Cenotaph Road opened.

The waves receded from around him. Lan didn't simply let loose. He maintained control as long as possible, nurturing the energy, stroking it as if it were a thing alive, coaxing the most possible from it. The cenotaph had been opened to another world, but an important element still remained.

Inyx.

"Come closer. Come to me. Follow the light from the Cenotaph Road," he called into the whiteness.

"Lan, so near. I'm coming. Wait for me. Wait!"

"Inyx!"

He blinked and stared into the yawning crypt carved into the stone altar. A misty form appeared, shimmered, started to vanish. He *reached* out and manipulated the energies and prevented Inyx's departure. The form coalesced into a woman. She lay in the crypt, confusion on her face. She turned, tried to sit up. The narrow confines prevented her from doing more than straightening her long legs.

"Inyx, you're back. Thank all . . . Inyx!"

"Lan!"

She reached out, touched his hand, then disappeared with a loud snapping noise.

"What happened? Krek, she was here and I lost her. She's back in the mist."

"No, friend Lan Martak. She didn't go back. I watched carefully. She retained her material body, and, by human standards, a nice one it is, too. I prefer more fur on the legs, naturally. All arachnids enjoy the sight of several well-turned legs, those being our most prominent feature."

"Krek!"

"Oh, yes. She formed most nicely, then winked out. I do believe the cenotaph took her. She walked the Road."

"It opened already? Of course it did. I opened it!"

"And it has already closed. Remember, the cenotaphs do not remain open constantly. Only once daily do they open, then for an appallingly short period. You should look into changing that, the next cenotaph you make."

"It's closed?" Lan hardly believed his ears. The first crypt he'd entered had been open to another world for only seconds. This one consecrated to Ehznoll had been open for long minutes—but he'd taken those minutes to summon Inyx, to coax her from the whiteness. By the time she'd reposed in the crypt, the time had expired.

Inyx went ahead of them to a new world. They had to wait for another day to follow.

"We're still not together!" he complained.

"There is only time between the two of you now," said Morto. "Wait a day, then follow. She saw you and must know that you follow. She will wait at the other side."

"Wait," said Lan glumly. "So we wait."

"The time is almost upon us," said Krek. "Prepare to follow Inyx."

"I'm ready," said Lan. "Are you, Morto?"

"No."

"What?"

"I'm not going." The mage's son stood to one side of the hut, his chin held high and a glow about him that Lan had seen before. He appeared more confident now, his shoulders straighter and his face more composed. For too long he had lived in his father's long shadow. Morto obviously had come to a decision on his own now, possibly for the first time. Free of familial obligation, he grew as a man.

"Why not?"

"I will stay on this world. Others offer me nothing I can't find here."

"And?"

"I would carry on Ehznoll's religion. The strength of this cenotaph is a tribute to his courage. There must have been parts of his belief more potent than any magic. Perhaps faith is always stronger. It is something I must explore for my own peace of mind. Also, my father lies on this mountain; I think my destiny does, also."

"Come with us, Morto. Don't spend your life in this way. Help us continue your father's fight against Claybore."

"My fight lies elsewhere. I haven't the talent or will to do battle with Claybore. Let me stay and tend to this holy shrine. It is something I can do, something I want to do. Go, go find your friend."

"The cenotaph opens, friend Lan Martak."

"Morto?"

"Go."

Lan's blossoming magical sense "saw" the cenotaph begin to open. It glowed like a brightly lit doorway. Krek momentarily blocked off the light, then vanished. Through the illuminated rectangle Lan saw another world, a startlingly different world. He glanced back at Morto to see a different kind of light, a religious fervor such as had sent Ehznoll to his death.

But it wasn't death Lan Martak sought. It was life. Life and Inyx and freedom. He dropped into the crypt, felt the magics work on him and send him into another world, a world to be warned of Claybore and his grey-clad soldiers, a world of boundless promise—and boundless evil.

He faded from Mount Tartanius and awoke to the next step along the Cenotaph Road.

MORE SCIENCE FICTION! ADVENTURE